To! Jo.

OL' SLANTFACE

From the grandson of the Old Duke.

John T. Wayne

John T. Wayne

3-25-17

The Gaslight Boys Series

THE NEW STANDARD IN WESTERN
FOLKLORE!

OL' SLANTFACE

John T. Wayne

Mockingbird Lane Press

Ol' Slantface
Copyright © 2014 John T. Wayne

Mockingbird Lane Press—Maynard, Arkansas

ISBN: 978-1-6341532-2-5

Library of Congress Control Number: 2014954792

0 9 8 7 6 5 4 3 2 1

www.mockingbirdlanepress.com
Graphic art cover: Jamie Johnson

THE GASLIGHT BOYS

From 1861 – 1865 a storm rolled through our nation and in its wake left behind a path of death and destruction. Over 100,000 children lost everything they had come to know including both parents. This tragedy took place during the Civil War and sadly for years after; during a period known as Reconstruction. What became of those children? How were they instrumental in shaping the future of our society? These questions are answered in my series of books called, "The Gaslight Boys." Charles Dickens is credited with being the original Gaslight Boy, but there were many other Gaslight Children created by the war. The Gaslight Boys series brings to life the hardships, the conditions and individual struggles buried and /or forgotten by time.

These are the stories of the young men and women who grew up to become great in their own right, men and women of the great society. Some of them became great, some became outlaws, and some died short of the chance. The Gaslight Boy novels are their stories.

---John T. Wayne

WHEN PAST MEETS PRESENT!

I have read the detailed accounts of Pony Express witnesses, such as the one by John D. Young of Chicago; he wrote in his journal all which happened as he saw the events unfold. There are others, but the way in which everyone has chosen to highlight the event gives thinking writers pause. The question remains; who was the first rider, for there is no description or mention of the man until forty years after the fact, (a tall tale told by a known drunk)? It was as if no reporter could chronicle the truth, or swallow the bitter pill if you will. The newspapers of the day could not comment on the one portion of the story they so dearly wanted to report on. The first rider being black held all reporters and witnesses mute.

Russell, Majors and Waddell had advertised heavily for orphans. How much more expendable were you as a young black orphan? There are considerations here, and although I am not one to rewrite history, I assure you there could have been no other explanation. America was looking for a Hero, America needed a Hero, and the new venture provided by the Pony Express would produce one. So Russell, Majors and Waddell, not wanting to have a kid outclass the masterminds and financial brain trust behind the impossible project, (for no one thought they could actually do it), or be held in higher esteem, they did the only thing which made sense. They mounted a young black boy who was very good with horses. His name was Nat Love.

The fact is; there are no stories written by the newspapers the first week of April 1860 which describe the rider who rode out that day. The story conveniently dries up after the mail arrives on the train ride from Hannibal to St Joe.   --John T. Wayne

This book is dedicated to my Uncle John, Uncle Wayne Morris, my Aunt Mary Ann, Uncle Bobby, and Aunt Pat.

A father's love must include correction,
or it is no love at all.

John T. Wayne

Chapter 1

Being an older brother was not my choice. When you're born, you don't get to choose your circumstances in life and you certainly don't get to choose your family. On that note I can tell you one thing I had learned since coming into this world. A youngster starts making decisions long before he or she has any idea how the teeny-tiniest of choices can screw up their life or for how long.

My name is Dillon Childs, and as a guardian at the age of twelve, scurrying under the gaslights lining the streets of St. Louis with the War Between the States well underway, I was receiving a crash course in decision making. Good or bad, it was apparent some decisions haunted you for the rest of your life. Up to that point, mine seemed to be of the questionable variety and I was hoping they wouldn't hound me anywhere near my whole life; but the odds against some sort of reprieve in the decision-making department seemed almighty slim.

St. Louis had not been the best decision on my father's part, for Uncle Sebastian was nowhere to be found and the streets were already filled with homeless children when my little sister and I arrived. The war had been under way for more than a year, and 1863 as it now stood, was shaping up to be a time of desperation for the

Southern States and the Childs' family. I had no skills to speak of which would allow me to get a job. I was too young to hold one anyway. At twelve-years-old, I had my work cut out for me.

Jenny was my little sister and what made matters worse, when I made a wrong decision it didn't just impact me; my lack of experience affected her life too. Dillon Childs was all she had to look after her and she was only six. I hated what had happened and how we'd ended up here, but there was nothing I could do to change what had led to our circumstance. Jenny was my charge and I wasn't doing very well at that moment in time. She was always hungry, but didn't complain too much, for she saw I was hungry too. She understood to a degree, but there were times when she just wouldn't stop whining.

To our credit, we were able to catch fish and eat frog legs when our luck was really down and out, but only because Pa had taught me how to run a line and gig a frog from the age of five. We had been born under the rim of a deep blue-ridge overlooking the prettiest waterfalls a body ever saw, under the trees where the dusk turns the hills blue and purple of an evening. Ours had been a land of unsurpassed wild game and cool rushing waters down which the Current River flowed. Of a morning there was usually some type of critter watering itself in the river, and an easier table setting was never had. Those were the good old days for which I now longed. Good old days for a twelve-year-old boy and his six-year-old sister; her life only just begun.

Current River had been our home until two weeks ago. Ma had passed on just after giving birth to Jenny, but not from giving birth; she died from being bitten by a copperhead. Pa had done a sight of work to raise us from then on, but now the Civil War was gathering a full head of steam and our little home was no longer safe according to Mr. Childs. Pa finally relented and signed up to fight for the Confederacy, instructing me to head for St. Louis, where I would find my Uncle Sebastian. Having never met the man, I wasn't sure just how I was supposed to get in touch with him, but Pa had said his last name was the same as ours, and he looked a good deal like Pa himself. I had the address Pa had given me, but the house was empty when we arrived.

Now after three lonely days living on the streets of the Gateway City, I'd discovered Uncle Sebastian had gone and done just like Pa; he had joined the Confederacy to fight the Yankees. What struck me odd about St. Louis was the fact I hadn't seen a Confederate soldier in those three days. Every soldier I had seen wore the Yankee dark blue, and there were a'plenty of them about. I soon learned this was because of a place called Jefferson Barracks, where the North was signing up soldiers to fight, training them before shipping them off to war. With no prospects for an easy meal, I told Jenny we were going back home to our cabin in the woods and we headed south out of town on the river road that fourth morning, just walking.

"Where's our wagon," Jenny asked.

"It's already gone, we've got to walk," I said.

"I don't want to walk," she whined.

Things were shaping up for disaster, but I really had no idea how bad a Childs disaster might become.

I knew how to fix cornpone, I knew how to string a rabbit and I knew how to catch fish or gig a frog. I had no intention of becoming part of the rabble I had just witnessed upon the streets of St. Louis. I had no desire to watch my sister grow up begging for a handout for want, or lack of proper care, and what I'd witnessed was no place for a lady or a young girl. Jenny would be abused by those boys sooner or later if we stayed among them, and then I would have to kill me somebody sure.

Death had been riding me hard for the last few years, and I don't mean my own, but the fact I would sooner or later have to kill someone for something they would do to my family. I couldn't say who, where or when, I couldn't even explain my feelings, but the Grim Reaper sure seemed to be riding my coat-tail awful hard these days. A young man of twelve could do without such desperate thoughts, but I surely was having them.

Our ride north to St. Louis had been easy, for Pa had fixed us up with a friend of his who was committed to seeing us all the way to town. Once we arrived however, he cut us loose like the unwanted baggage we had been to him. He had fixed for us, and taken care to see we got through all right, but that was as far as the man's promise to Pa went, and when we landed on the wharf that was the last we saw of Mr. Jeremiah Culpepper, and him supposed to be a Christian minister and all.

He had gotten his supplies and left town the same day, so he had a three day head start on us. With him in a buckboard and us on foot there was no hope of catching up with the man. Not that I wanted to; my being so young and inexperienced I just naturally thought there was something terrible wrong with the preacher man, but that was just to my way of thinking. I had not one ounce of proof in the matter, yet the man hadn't said two words the entire trip to St. Louis. His evil stare had been an unsettling thing, but an evil stare is not exactly indisputable evidence of the devil in a man. That's what I believed at the time. I couldn't have been more wrong, but that's one of those things a kid has to learn the hard way.

As we walked the river road, Jenny began to complain about her tired little legs, but I had naught for an answer. I pressed her to walk as far as she could. I carried her piggyback for a ways, then I set her down and she walked again. By the time dusk arrived I was whipped—not just whipped—but beaten, tumbledown and crippled from carrying Jenny so much. I never knew a young man's body could hurt as bad as mine, and what occurred to me was the fact I could not make the trip home in such a manner. We would never survive, at least I wouldn't, and under these conditions if I failed, so did Jenny.

I found some tall grass along the roadway which deer had slept the previous night and we made a soft bed underneath the stars and went to sleep. I was out like a light and when I came to, there was someone sitting on horseback talking with another person out on the road about twenty yards away. I checked Jenny and she was well-nigh dead with fatigue, so she was not going to wake up at the sound of two strangers talking. I, on the other hand, couldn't help but wish forevermore that I had been as dead to the world as she was that night, for what I heard was pure evil, and from the moment I overheard the conversation I knew I could not ignore the matter.

"Listen, Jake, dem kids got no home, no folks' and no way to fend for dem-selves. I's don't care how you get 'em, but I's want thirty-sev'n ta fo'ty all tied up n' ready ta set sail by dis time next month. I need 'em shipboard no later dan full moon down at de rendezvous point on de Miss-nippy. Den we sail under de full moon fo' New Orleans where dey's a freighter a'waitin' ta take every man Jack of 'em an' make sailors out of 'em, or dey's die tryin'. I's get two hundred a head fo' anything big enough ta pull anchor, so de bigger dey is da better. You got dat?"

"Yes Sir, boss."

"You's bring me one extry ta hep wit de cookin', hear me? I's don' care if it's a girl or boy, but dey's better be able ta whirl a fry pan, understand?"

"All right, Lucifer," Jake resounded.

"Now get along," the one called Lucifer instructed.

The underling, whoever Jake was, turned his mount back in the direction of St. Louis and galloped away, leaving a cloud of dust hanging thick and heavy in the cool night air along the darkened roadway. From the center-pocket of his overalls, the Boss, the man called Lucifer, pulled a tobacco pouch and stuffed his pipe full. Just as the boss-man began to turn his horse about, he lit a match and I caught a glimpse of his features and cringed inwardly. His face was slanted in a God-awful fashion and his eyes appeared to be slanted at near the same angle, with one sunken and one protruding as if his face had been split open and patched back together unsuccessfully, revealing the meanest looking black man I ever did see. His match died out and Jenny moved in her sleep. I cupped my hand over her mouth to shush her because far as I could tell, Lucifer was the Devil himself.

"Shhhhhhh," I whispered to Jenny.

"Who dat," his demon-like voice bellowed into the night. He dropped his match and snaked a pistol out of the holster he wore around his overalls. I held my breath and lay perfectly still. I did put the available finger of my right hand to my lips indicating to Jenny she needed to be silent as we stared one another directly in the eyes, for he had awakened her. If she squealed at all, we were done for.

"Who dat out dere," the boss-man demanded in no uncertain terms. "You's come ow'd here dis minute or I's..." his words trailed off. Jenny and I stared into one another's eyes helplessly, afraid to make any move which might beget a sound. We stared and held our breath. Just then a jackrabbit jumped from near our position and spirited away across the meadow, bounding this way and that for all it was worth. I was certain the fellow had been just about ready to strike another match and nudge his horse in our direction, but the rabbit spared us.

A chuckle and then, "I's gettin' jumpy," Lucifer observed out loud. With no warning the terrifying black man turned his horse back to the south, holstered his weapon and rode away, leaving us trembling in the tall grass. Behind him he left the sweet aroma of pipe tobacco drifting through the air. My nostrils took a deep whiff of the pleasant aroma and I exhaled. The man seemed to smoke a very good tobacco. I wondered what kind, how much it cost and so on. How could a black man afford such a luxury as tobacco? Blacks were slaves, weren't they?

I knew we had to move because if the man became suspicious and began to second guess himself, he might come back and search for us yet again. We waited until he was well out of hearing and then got up from our comfortable bed and headed towards the woods on the other side of the meadow; the same direction the rabbit had run.

At the edge of the tree line the grass was again tall and soft when laid over or pressed down, so we made a new bed near an evergreen next to a tall old pecan tree. Doing so reminded me that Ma used to bake a pecan pie before she passed on, and suddenly I knew I was going to try and bake one just as soon as I could lay my hands on the necessary spices and sugar. I was suddenly devoted to the notion as soon as we could get back to our cabin on Current River. Of course, I had no idea how long that was going to take. I figured a few days, but life had charted a different course for the likes of Dillon Childs.

Thinking back to the conversation I'd overheard, I realized I was going to have to make up my mind any old day now. Those men out there on the road were bad men with evil intentions. If I had any doubts, they were erased as soon as Ol' Slantface started yelling. His voice was deep and raspy, just like I would have figured the devil's voice might sound, almost that of a toad frog. Had the rabbit not jumped and ran when it did, I would have. That meant we would surely have been caught and would now be in the clutches of the kidnapper. Who was the man called boss that looked as if he'd met up with the wrong end of an axe? One thing was certain; he was not a white man. Could black men trade slaves too?

Slave trading was, after all, what the war seemed to be about now that Lincoln had delivered his Emancipation Proclamation. If the man could no longer deliver slaves to and from buyers, might he not look for another market? Dealing in human flesh seemed to fit the personality of Ol' Slantface, but then what I knew of men was little enough. How could I, a young boy, judge such a man's character? Maybe it was only me he scared half to death. I had little to go on, yet he had said he could get two hundred dollars a head for those big enough to weigh anchor. What did two hundred dollars times forty add up to? I could figure some with the smaller numbers, but these were more than I had ever attempted to cipher. One thing was for sure and certain; it was more money than I was likely to see in my lifetime.

At sunup the following morning we began to walk. Once again we headed south, only this time I stayed clear of the road. If those fellows were going to be looking for children who might fit the bill, I had no intention of delivering myself up to them unexpectedly. I had Jenny to watch out for, which was all the more reason for me to be cautious, keeping out of clearings and off the roads.

We traveled light that day, only I was able to find some wild blackberries, and ripe they were. I'm afraid the two of us made quite a mess of ourselves while gorging on the hapless fruit, some of which wasn't ripe yet. After having our fill, we laid down again for a mid-day nap and dozed under a big whispering willow. We were well off of the road and in the edge of the tree line.

I heard a low drone for several minutes before I recognized what was causing it. Then I saw the horses as they ascended the river road. There were hundreds of them coming up from down by the river, heading north toward St. Louis. Blue-bellies they were, mounted on horseback, drawing wagons with mules and oxen pulling cannons. For more than an hour we sat transfixed at the edge of the forest watching the Federals while they sojourned by as one long column far as the eye could see in either direction.

Presently the end of the column drew near, quicker than I had expected because the dust created by the horse soldiers had masked the end of the procession. The last soldiers looked more gray than blue because of all the dust which had settled upon their horses and uniforms. As the remainder of the troop disappeared from sight, I got Jenny up and we skedaddled, zigzagging through the trees in a southerly direction headed toward our home.

Along about dusk I smelled wood-smoke from a fire and we halted. I told Jenny to stay put while I checked on the source of the smell. Slowly I crept up to the ridgeline before me and peeked over. It was Ol' Slantface, with two other men who didn't present any better an honest figure. The three were roasting squirrel and rabbit over a small open flame. I licked my lips and wondered just how I could get me some of their meal without getting caught.

Have you ever had such a foolish idea that you believed in it all the more? That's exactly the kind of thoughts I was having as I witnessed their charbroiled meat roasting over an open flame, with me and Jenny nursing a four day hunger.

Looking about, I could see where their horses were tethered, and a plan began formulating in the back of my mind. If I could sneak down there and spook their horses enough to run them off, I'd likely have a free hand with their evenings fixing's. The sun had gone behind the ridge, leaving me more in the dark than not. Slowly I began to ease my way down toward their horses. Though they were unsaddled, the bits remained in their mouths, and I marveled when I got to them, for they were out of sight from half the camp. I jumped on the back of one, taking the reins, and slapped the other two on the rump and lit a shuck for the river, southeast away from the meanest bunch of men I'd seen in my short lifetime. I heard yelling and shouting behind me and a pistol shot rang through the evening air. The other two horses seemed to want to stay with the horse I was aback of, and suddenly I wasn't thinking about food anymore. The idea occurred to me that we now had transportation.

With effort, I leaned over and grabbed the reins of one of the other horses and headed in a wide sweeping circle back to where Jenny was waiting for me. When I got to the spot I had left her, she was nowhere to be found. Cursing my luck, I began to wonder what had happened to her. If those men had found her, she was in trouble and so was I, because I'd not abandon her.

Dismounting in a grove of trees where I would be concealed by their bulk, I once again eased up the ridge and peeked over. My eyes widened at the sight, but I should have known what would happen before I ever conceived my foolish notion. Jenny was sitting there pretty as you please, eating a fine meal all by herself, her reflection unmistakable in the firelight. Looking hastily about the camp I saw no one else. The men were obviously out searching for their horses.

Suddenly I saw a slight movement off to my left, and with a start, identified Ol' Slantface staring directly at my little sister, the firelight glowed in his eyes revealing the insanity within. He wasn't moving any more than need be, and spotting him had been pure luck, because he was black as the ace of spades, allowing the darkness to cloak him in a kindred veil. He stood there watching as Jenny put away their meager supper. I knew right then I was in more trouble than a boy had a right to be. He had her pegged and he was going to catch her red handed. If I stayed or tried to save her, they'd get their hands on me too.

Cautiously, I backed away from the ridge and mounted up a good hundred yards away. Taking the reins of the two extra horses, I began to slowly ride in a circle around the camp taking care to be as quiet as possible. Suddenly it occurred to me I needed to be making all kinds of noise, which might draw the men away from Jenny. I started yelling, "Giddy up, come on horse, let's go," and such like. I finally reached the road and began to gallop toward the south, for my intended distraction had not moved Ol' Slantface one bit. Lucifer and his minions were going to have my little sister in short order. I just prayed they didn't eat her.

Without a horse among them, I knew they would be headed for Pevely or some close settlement thereabouts, and I knew they wouldn't hurt an innocent little girl such as Jenny. In fact, I thought she might eat better with them for the time being. I knew she would be scared, but she would be all right. I, on the other hand, was now a horse thief!

Such unexpected realization did nothing to comfort me. Pa had always told me what became of horse thieves; how they were hung, usually without any kind of trial. Funny, I hadn't even let the thought cross my mind until I actually had the horses in my possession. Did they hang twelve-year-old boys for a horse thief? Something told me I didn't want to know.

I rode south a ways, then made camp for the night well off the roadway, up in the trees, but only when I had traveled far enough to know for certain the men who had my sister could not cover the distance between us before I awoke the following morning. I had no fire, no food and no way to get any. Jenny at least had eaten. I was happy for her. I staked all three horses so they could crop grass, yet couldn't run off, then lay back to sleep.

My mind raced with thoughts of Jenny, and what Ol' Slantface might do to her. If he was the devil, I knew I would forever rue the day, but I was gambling that he was merely a mortal man. I had stolen his only mode of transportation, there were soldiers all about and they seemed to be Blue-bellies. The man was not going to thank me for setting them afoot. I fell asleep wondering if I had done the right thing, worrying about Jenny.

Chapter 2

A bright but doubt-filled day began to unfold as I led my cluster of stolen horses down the long straight road which flanked the Mississippi River on the Missouri side. I was out of the hill country, down in the lower bottoms, the part local folks called the delta. There are those who would argue that the delta was much farther south in Louisiana, but such an argument never made much sense to me; I didn't know what the word delta meant and didn't care. As far as I was concerned, anyone who wanted a delta could have one, because most of the time it seemed to be under water anyway. Sometimes in springtime the Mississippi River was eight and ten miles wide in places.

From time to time the going was questionable at best, but I was in no hurry. I had no intention of letting those men get completely away from me, for they had my little sister and I was going to keep an eye on her. I was leading them like hogs to slaughter, but in my mind I was never so sure of my plans, for I had nothing with which to slaughter them.

I was quietly going out of my mind with thoughts and worry for Jenny. For the last few hours, I had been letting the men who had her come close to me, just close enough for them to see me riding with their horses, and then I would scamper off and put more distance between us.

I knew how they were getting along. I had seen them carrying Jenny on their shoulders, taking turns. As one man tired another one would take over. From time to time I let them get close enough to see me real good, but never so close as to be in any danger from gunfire. I simply wanted to keep them moving in my direction. Today was going to be a hot and sultry spring day at best, with the threat of a good spring rain hanging in the air, so I made certain to water the horses frequently while keeping an eye over my shoulder.

About noon, as I sat watering the three mounts, I realized the men no longer had Jenny with them. What had they done with her? Where could she be? As I sat my horse, I could hear the thunder roll off in the distance. The clouds were beginning to build, and if my guess was right we were fixing to get a good old fashioned gully washer. I waited right where I was, for I wanted answers. At length Ol' Slantface drew within about fifty yards of me.

"Where's my sister?" I yelled just as lightning speared from the sky. The storm was getting closer.

"She's waitin' fo' ya. Say's she won' go no further wi'out her broth'uh."

"I don't believe you. You did something with her," I accused.

"Look-a-here boy, I's don' go round hurting chil'ren, neither o' you's in any danger. Let us have de hosses back an' you's can have yo sister," he explained with his incredible southern accent.

"Why can't I have her anyway?"

"Cause ya little thief, you done stole our hosses. Dat's a hanging offense."

"You plan to hang me?" I yelled back.

"We ain't a'goin' to hang no body, but you sho' got' ta give de hosses back. We needs 'em," the man argued convincingly.

"How do I know you'll honor your word to let me have my sister back?"

"I's gib ya de girl first," Ol' Slantface offered, as he was now within twenty yards.

"That's far enough," I said. He took another look at me and stopped in his tracks. Had Lucifer come any closer, I was set to spur my horse and take off again, although I had no such thing as a set of spurs. Because he stopped, we were now at an impasse.

"You's got no reason to fear me boy, I's jus-a travelin' man. Why, I could'a shot you by now if'n I'd wanted to hurt you." Pausing, he continued, "Now, if'n you'll get down and let me have dem hosses back, you and little sister can be on yo' way," the disfigured fellow promised.

I didn't trust him in any way shape or nohow, but they had my sister and it was my duty to get her back. My belly was rubbing my backbone, and to make the situation worse, Ol' Slantface pulled a polished red apple out of his pocket and began peeling it with his pocket knife right in front of me. Where the devil he got a red apple from I didn't figure to ever know, but I knew Pa had kept a stash of them down in the root cellar back home. Stood to reason other folks could do the same. Had me wondering what root cellar the man had robbed.

"Give me my sister and you'll have your horses," I told him.

"Go back'n git de girl!" Slantface yelled back at his men. One of them turned back and the other kept coming. "What's your name, son?"

"Dillon Childs," I answered.

"You'd make a real good soldier. Which side ya pullin' fo'?"

"My Pa is fighting for the south. I suppose the Confederacy would be good enough for me."

"Dog-gone son, we's on de same side of things; why don't you get down. I's see to it you an' little sister get to where it is you's goin' an de two o'you won't starve. I's got a crack shot and won't anybody travelin' in my party go hungry." Then he took a bite of his freshly peeled apple.

I still didn't trust the man, but my stomach was saying give the man half a chance, you can't be any worse off than you are right now. That was my stomach doing the talking. I had different feelings altogether, but my stomach won the argument. When I saw Jenny cut loose and come running towards me, I got down and walked over to the man I knew only as Lucifer, or as I preferred, Ol' Slantface, a name I daren't mention in front of him.

"I reckon I let my fear get the better of me, mister. When I saw you had my sister, I thought I had no choice but to run off with your horses. When I saw how you left them picketed I just naturally took them. I'm sorry."

As I reached out my hand with the reins lying across my palm offering him back his horses, he slapped me hard on the jaw and I went down in a heap. While I lay on the ground staring up at him, he picked up the horses' reins from the ground and looked down upon me. "Let dat be a lesson, Dillon. Some men don't want an apology, dey want you ta pay. Dey want ta see you squirm 'cause dey hearts is filt with hate and rage. Don't ever apologize ta no man son, it's a sign of weakness," he said. Reaching down, he offered me a hand up.

I turned my head to see Jenny had stopped her approach; she had come to a sudden halt, so I decided to accept this man's hand. He lifted me back to my feet and handed me my own fresh red apple, then he turned to his oncoming partners. "You'ns rides back and git de saddles. Me and de chil-ren'll be right over dare under dat big shade tree waitin' fo' ya," he said as he handed his men the reins to all three horses.

Now, I had seen many things in my first twelve years on earth, mostly in the last two, but I never did see no colored man giving orders to a white man, let alone two of them.

At that moment lightning slit the sky just over the hill to the south, the storm was getting closer. I noticed a riverboat on the old Mississippi and suddenly wished I was on it. There I would be safe from the likes of such men as these who were with us now. On the river I knew my way around, but a lad my age would want for enough money to buy passage. Pa had always paid my way in bygone days. I watched as two columns of black smoke puffed out of the stacks, drifting off to disappear into the waiting blue abyss. Suddenly, Jenny was there beside me, wrapping her arms around me. She was scared and showing it.

"Dat's de Natchez steamin' her way to St. Louie no doubt, she'll be docking on de wharf in a couple hours,"

Ol' Slantface said. "Now son, where's it you and ya sistah wants to go?" he asked as politely as he was ever going to. I had a suspicion whenever Ol' Slantface asked a question it was usually with an underlying authority, this question being no exception.

"We want to go home to our cabin on Current River."

"Well now, Dillon Childs, yes, yes now I see," he offered as he rubbed his shifting jawbone. "Dat's good a place as any ta wait fo' my men. You got a Ma or Pa somewhere?"

"Like I said, Pa is fighting for the Confederacy. Ma died six years ago." Jenny began to cry as I said it, so I pulled her closer and told her everything would be all right.

He took a long look at Jenny and no one needed to tell me he was putting two and two together. He knew well what had happened without asking. He also seemed to know more than he was letting on, but how much more I could not guess. What could the man possibly know about me and my sister? We had just met, but something in the man's expression had shown a realization of some kind. What he realized I might never know, but with folded arms he continued to rub an invisible beard.

Finally, after a rather distracting delay, he dropped his arms.

"Dillon, if'n you will allow me, I's take care of you young'uns. I's no married man myself and I cain't hep what life has done ta me, but if'n you'll give me a half-square deal I's do fo' ya until your Pa comes home from de war. I's make sho no one bothers you kids. Pact?" he said, sticking out his big paw for me to shake.

Now this here man looked forevermore like the devil himself to me, but the last thing I wanted to do was give him reason to shorten my time on earth and send me to hell. I took his oversize paw and we shook, not because I wanted to, but I was afraid he'd slap me silly again if I didn't. I was leery, for my gut was telling me I had just shaken hands with Satan. My suspicions were he would use us for as long as he wanted or as long as things made sense and then do away with us altogether when he no longer needed us. I was big enough to help weigh anchor, so I considered what he had said back there on the road in the middle of the night and I didn't feel safe in any case. He'd sell me down river right along with the others, and then what would become of Jenny? I had no proof to back up my suspicion, all I had was my gut feeling, but my intuition was a strong one. Ol' Slantface was the meanest man I'd ever met. Why, he ranked right up there next to our preacher, Jeremiah Culpepper...now, why would I make a comparison like that? Jeremiah Culpepper was a well-respected preacher in our community. Well, at least Ol' Slantface talked, I reassured myself.

It was a good camp Ol' Slantface had picked out for us, and after watching the man shoot our unexpected groceries, I decided I had better not get him angry at me for any reason. As we were walking toward the tree he had picked out for our camp, a turkey flew up straight across our path. As fast as the thought came to me that such a bird would make for a nice supper, he jerked his six-shooter from his holster and pulled the trigger. With one bullet, he shot the turkey on the fly. Our fresh-killed bird fell into a nose dive, crashing headlong into a downed log, and if the bullet hadn't killed the fowl, the breaking of his neck on the hollow log would have. We had our supper before I was able to finish my thought.

"Go's fetch dat bird, Dillon. We's gonna eat good tonight," he proclaimed.

I didn't argue with the man. He had shot the bird with what appeared to be an automatic reflex. The least I could do was carry the spoils to our campsite. Maybe I was just impressed because I never saw my own father pull off a shot like that, or maybe because I was just a kid, but either way I understood one thing from that day forward. I never wanted to be the target in front of this man's gun. Not even if I was a full grown man, had a gun of my own and the odds appeared to be even, because I'm telling you, they wouldn't be.

I gathered the wood necessary for a fire while Ol' Slantface de-feathered and dressed our winged supper. The storm seemed to be passing to the south, so I watched what he did and it was slick. He slit the bird's throat and then cut it right up the neck to the belly. Then he stood on the birds head, gripped the skin he had peeled back and yanked real hard. Turkey bird was skinned that quick, wings, breast and all right down to its feet. I wanted to eat it just as fast, but a turkey cooks slowly over an open fire, a fact I could not change. As a result, both Jenny and I had fallen asleep hungry, only to be wakened in the middle of the evening so we could eat. Ol' Slantface might be a hard man, but he wasn't going to let us starve any time soon.

"You chil'ren set up ta some meat," he said as the firelight flickered in his eyes. "I's had my fill and what's left won't be near so good, if'n you wait till morning." He had cut off chunks of breast meat and we each had a leg between us. Before we could finish eating our bird, my stomach was rumbling like it hadn't eaten in a month. I didn't know what to think, but I had no trouble lying back down and going to sleep, letting my stomach settle while I dreamed.

My dreams came to me in the form of nightmares. Someone was always pulling a gun on me, trying to make me do something I knew to be wrong. I never did capitulate to my knowledge, but to my way of thinking this was the cause of all my problems. I just didn't want to do what I was being told to do at gunpoint. Every unsavory character I could dream up was coming after me in my sleep, rooting around in dark places, searching for Dillon Childs so they might kill him. I even had a spot where I had a shooting target stuck on my forehead beneath my hat. I only remember that because someone had shot my hat off my head, revealing the mark. I awoke in a cold sweat, Ol' Slantface just sitting there staring at me.

Now, there was no way the slave trader could do anything about what his face had become. He looked mean even when he was smiling at me. I studied him for a moment and realized he was doing just that. He was deep in his own thoughts, not really paying me any mind. While his stare was in my direction, it was not directly at me. He looked mean as all git out, but suddenly I understood, he could do nothing about his appearance. He scared people, especially little children, but I was beginning to see a more reasonable side to him beneath his patchwork of threatening features.

After a bit more thought, I turned over and slept some more. This time as I dreamed, visions of Dillon Childs pulling off such a stunt like the shooting of our turkey kept playing over and over in my head. I was an ace marksman, able to shoot whatever I aimed at, but that was in my dreams. I never missed a target or the bull's-eye in my dreams. I shot with a long rifle, a pistol and sometimes two.

Duals were the common method for settling a dispute during the War Between the States, but in my dreams, there was no marching off ten paces then turning to fire. In my dreams, a gunfight would come off unexpectedly, but I was always the victor looking down upon my victim with pity at the end of each unwanted fight. Unwanted? How could a man ever end up in such a position? I filed the dreams away as child's play, but my gunfight dreams were always there haunting me as if trying to warn me of my future.

Jenny and I got up a couple of hours later while it was still dark and ate like a couple of piglets at slop time. I mean we devoured the rest of that turkey and went night-night faster than you can say "boogity, boogity." When we awoke the next morning, the others were back with all the gear they had abandoned on account of yours truly.

Mounting up, I rode behind Clayton Long and Jenny rode in front of Clifton Jackson. Clay and Cliff for short. I soon learned the name of Ol' Slantface was Lucifer Deal and the men called him Old Scratch sometimes. I learned while on our journey that a resentful slave being boarded in South Africa had swiped a machete across his face when he was younger, slicing his face clear off. It had been put back on as best the ship's doctor could manage, but the scar would be borne for the rest of his life. His face sagged to one side, and he had no feeling or control over his facial expression on that side, which was one reason his speech wasn't so good.

We made good time once we were on horseback, and in just a few days Jenny and I were almost home. When we entered the valley which had been my home all of my life, I saw smoke rising from our chimney and my heart gave a leap. My thought was Pa had returned home from the war already, but I soon realized my hopes were in vain. As we neared the cabin, Jeremiah Culpepper, the preacher who had delivered us to St. Louis, came to the front door and lit up with as evil a smile as I ever did see. He was standing in our cabin doorway and I couldn't for the life of me figure out why he should be in our house. He was our preacher, but that didn't give him no right to occupy our home, not as far as I could tell it didn't.

"What'd you bring them back for?" he admonished Ol' Slantface.

"Its best dey here wid us whilst we take care of business," Ol' Slantface responded. "I's don't want no trouble. 'Side's you'd know more' bout what to do wid 'em den I will."

"Throw a rope around their neck, tie a rock to the other end and drown them in the river unless you don't want no end of trouble," the preacher advised.

With the preacher's sudden advice, abject fear for my life and Jenny's sent a shiver of terror down my spine. This was the same man who had toted us all the way to St. Louis only a week earlier. Suddenly the thought occurred to me; just to get rid of us? He was talking as if he and Ol'

Slantface were of long-time acquaintances. I wondered just what such a declaration meant, but not for long.

"What are you doing in our cabin?" I spoke up.

"See what I mean? He's stirring up trouble already," Culpepper accused.

"Son, dey's a reason why de prea'cha in your cabin," Ol' Slantface answered. "Why, everybody knows dat a home will crumble to de ground much faster if'n its empty den if'n you have someone living inside. De prea'cha ain't doing no more den makin' sure de home is cared for properly an dat it don't crumble to de ground while your Pa is away. A home needs folks living in it in order ta last. If'n you didn't know dat, you do now."

I was watching the preacher as the man talked and the more Ol' Slantface spoke, the farther Culpepper's jaw dropped, and the cigar he was pulling on almost fell to the ground. I could tell that the man was in a state of disbelief as Old Scratch told me why our home needed to be occupied. I had no reason to doubt what the man was saying, yet the entire ramble seemed a deception to me. I couldn't guess why.

The cabin sat back from the riverbank about seventy-five yards to the east. It was a two story affair which Pa had built with plenty of hard work and grit. Jenny and I slept upstairs while our father had always slept downstairs. The cabin was fancy as most cabins go because Pa had put in a wooden floor, and a total of three rooms downstairs. The main living room sat one step higher than the other two rooms on either end of the house, but they all had finished wood floors. Pa had seen to the building of the "Log Cabin" before he ever went to call on Ma.

·"Well, now that we're home, there's no need for the preacher to stay," I offered in retort. I spoke directly to Lucifer, offering my opinion whether he wanted it or not.

"Nope, not if'n you can do de cookin' fo' everybody," Ol' Slantface corrected me and then added, "You might's want ta treat him respectful, cause you's goin' ta be his assistant."

Now it was my turn for my jaw to drop. I was no cook. I could catch game for dinner, but the cooking of it was another thing altogether. I could bake a pie, but that was all I'd learned to do. I steadied down a bit then and we dismounted.

"Dillon, be useful and put de hosses away," Slantface said as he handed me his reins. I gathered the others and headed for the barn. As I walked, it dawned on me that these men had been coming to our cabin all along. It was also abundantly clear that the preacher and these men knew one another. Just what was going on here? I was not sure; but our cabin was occupied by none other than Jeremiah Culpepper, the man who had given us a ride to St. Louis at my father's request. Something was amiss, yet I couldn't quite put my finger on it.

Where was Pa? He had skipped the first two years of the war, but now he'd signed up to fight, and I wondered where he might be fighting as I forked the horses some hay from the manger. Pa had said something about crossing the river and going down to Mississippi. Where in Mississippi? All I knew was, I wished I could locate him now. I had the feeling bad things were about to start happening which I would have no control over, and a boy my age had little he could count on when it came to stopping man-sized trouble. Picking up a brush, I began to curry the horses as I contemplated. The worst thing I could do was to stir up trouble for myself and Jenny, so I needn't do anything to get those men riled or angry at me. Jenny was counting on me as well, so I daren't do anything they might frown upon.

Somehow I had to get us away from here. Our home was where I wanted to be, but the place was no longer safe. It was occupied by ruffians of the worst kind, if I was to believe what I had overheard that night upon the road.

"Kidnapping," I suddenly said.

Where were they going to hold forty boys? As I glanced around our family barn, I knew. Our place had been the brute's intention all along. We were miles from any civilization and the barn would hide a large number of boys my age or bigger. Chains I had never seen, with big loops, already hung from the far wall; as if I needed such evidence to confirm my suspicion. Those men had ridden in here with little to no directions from me, which meant they already knew where our cabin was located. They hadn't even been surprised to see the preacher when they rode in, come to think of it, which meant they knew of one another from days gone by.

Had Uncle Sebastian not joined the southerners, Jenny and I would no doubt be safe and sound in his home somewhere in St. Louis, with no knowledge of what was taking place here. As I thought of that, I grasped the idea Jenny and I weren't in the plans these men had for the future. I realized what we were; unwanted contraband. Ol' Slantface recognized who I was the moment I introduced myself, that was why he gave us a ride all the way home, and his apple stash—I bet it had come from right here in our own cellar!

I would be sold into slavery along with the rest of the boys just as soon as the time came. How long did I have, a week, two? He must have felt I would be easier to deal with if he had me somewhere close by than if he didn't know where I was.

So, the preacher was their cook, if I was to believe them. How big was this operation? Ol' Slantface seemed to be their leader. There was Jeremiah Culpepper to cook, Clay and Cliff and some fellow named Jake, who I had not seen since that first night on the road outside the Gateway City. If they were going to transport forty young men from the streets of St. Louis, Jake would not be alone. No one needed to warn me of the trouble I was in. I was just the right age, ripe for being sold.

"What's taking you so long, boy?" it was Clay doing the asking as he stuck his head inside the barn door.

"I'm rubbing the horses down," I answered.

"All right, we were getting worried about you is all. Come on in to super when you're finished," he added and then turned for the house.

I guess I was taking a while longer than usual, but I liked horses and these three were some of the best I ever did see. I liked the big red one especially. I took my time on him and wondered just what I had gotten us into. Rubbing down the horses gave me a chance to think, time to plan and calm my nerves. Then I went inside to eat.

I hung my hat on the hat rack by the door as I entered, and then looked around.

"Where's Jenny?" I asked.

"She's in bed. Have a seat, Dillon, we need's ta talk," Slantface urged.

Sitting down to the plate Culpepper tossed in front of me, I dug in while Slantface talked. I listened and ate, but I was thinking too.

"Dis your home and I's don't want it said dat I's took advantage," he announced. "I's be fair and pay you fo' its use an' if'n you help out, I's can pay you wages while we's here. You have your sister ta look out fo'." He paused to let that part sink in. "I propose ta pay you a dollar a' day fo' rent on de place. I's throw in two bits fo' your help round de house. Dat's about forty dollars a month, Dillon. Do we have a deal?"

"If it's in advance," I spouted off without thinking.

"Why, the little reprobate," Jeremiah scolded as he dropped another plate on the table in front of Cliff. "It's a thief he is. I'm telling you, Lucifer, the boy is going to cause no end of trouble for us." Culpepper was incredulous. "Why don't you save your money and throw them both in the river?"

"I'm no thief and what's more this is my home," I argued. "I would like the money up front." All the while I knew Jeremiah Culpepper had young Dillon pegged. I was going to be no end of trouble for them. The only problem was, I had no earthly clue how much trouble I was capable of causing.

"Tell you what. I's give you de rent money up front cause dis is your home," Ol' Slantface agreed, "but I's hold your wages till you've earned 'em."

"That sounds fair to me," I remarked, figuring I wasn't going to get any better deal with Culpepper second guessing every offer the man made.

Taking a wad of cash from his overalls' center breast pocket, Ol' Slantface counted out thirty dollars and pushed it across the table toward me. Thirty dollars! I reached out to rake the cash my way, but Ol' Slantface grabbed my hand, then with his other he stabbed a knife into the tabletop right next to us.

"I takes my deals serious, young Dillon. I's honest, but I won't be wronged." He stared directly into my eyes then let go my hand.

I scraped my money off of the table and put it in my pocket then continued to eat, all the while thinking this was my last supper!

"It seems to me if we're going to feed the boy, we ought to get some of that back," Culpepper complained.

"Preacher man, I know how to catch game in this here valley a'plenty. I'll be putting meat on the table for you to eat. I'll not be paying you for that!" I spoke boldly but inside I was scared to death. I looked back at my fork which was beginning to shake in my hand so I got busy shoveling more food into my mouth in order to help mask my case of the jitters.

Ol' Slantface let out a laugh and bellowed so loud, I thought he was going to choke and die right there. He plucked his knife out of the table and put it away while he laughed. Cliff and Clay were laughing and smiling too. I didn't know what I had done that was so funny, but for the first time in days I smiled, and then I looked up at Culpepper and my frown returned immediately. The man hated me, and every wrinkle on his ugly face announced the fact. He was being laughed at, and I had been the cause of the laughter directed toward him. As bad as my situation seemed, I was beginning to have some fun of my own, but Culpepper was going to deal with me eventually. I knew he could not let a little boy have the upper hand. I had embarrassed him deeply and the look on his face meant one thing. I would pay dearly for my transgression.

I ate then, and when I finished I went to bed. I lay awake for a while unable to sleep. Although I couldn't hear plainly, I did overhear bits and pieces of what was to come.

"To trust me," was part of what I heard, and then, "no evidence."

What did it mean? There certainly wasn't much to go on. I was tired, but I struggled to try and figure what might happen next. I knew that sooner or later boys would start showing up; boys who would be my age and older, with no parents to speak of and no home. Not that I would know any of them. Which had me thinking, I had things pretty good here as long as I did my job and didn't get in the way. I wouldn't know those boys, so what difference did it make? Many of the boys I had witnessed on the streets of St. Louis would no doubt be better off with a good feeding every day. Who was I to deny them three squares or a chance to learn a good trade aboard a sailing ship?

Who was I kidding? I was a witness. Those men downstairs had to do away with me one way or another. Ol' Slantface or the preacher neither one would want my tongue wagging about the countryside telling people what I knew. I would be sold along with the rest of the boys, no two ways about it.

A meal or two every day was worth something, for I had just spent four days during the previous week fairly starving. I now knew what it meant to go without food. If the kidnapped boys were fed well, and they would be, who was I to interfere? They might appreciate a meal every day, even if they were chained to a wall. In St. Louis, I hadn't managed a meal the entire time I was there, and it was a big city with food on every street corner, although not unless you could pay for it. I hadn't stolen any, but the thought had crossed my mind that third day, before I decided we were going to go home.

At my age, I wasn't holding out much hope of getting out of this in any kind of shape, but my father had always said, no matter what, you've got to try. Well, I was no shakes at giving advice, but I had taken my fair share from time to time. One thing was for certain, I was going to try and do something, what was still a mystery.

Chapter 3

The following morning when I awoke, I dressed and headed to the barn. I figured to get my rabbit traps set and then drop a line in Current River where there was no end of channel cat. My father had always insisted they were good eating. There were also plenty of blue gill, perch, and carp up close to the bank. One way or another, I was going to earn my two bits a day.

I forked hay to the stock, and then cleaned out the manure and put it out by the garden Pa had always kept since Ma passed away. He had said manure would make the crops grow good and strong. I didn't pretend to know why, but as far as I could tell he'd been correct. I didn't see any reason not to do my chores just because we'd been set upon by brutes from the big city. I figured if I worked hard enough, those fellows might see some value in keeping me around. Not that I wanted to stay, but I sure-as-dickens didn't want to end up the same place those other boys were headed.

Once I was finished at the barn, I dug up a few of the smaller wild carrots and headed off into the woods. As I walked across the yard, Culpepper watched me from his perch on the front porch of our cabin with a fresh cigar dangling from his lips.

"Where you headed there, boy?" Culpepper used the word 'boy' with derision in his voice.

"If you want fresh meat, I'll need to bait my rabbit traps," I answered and kept walking. He eyed me as I made my way into the woods, and I knew he didn't trust me even one little bit, but I planned to make him and everyone else trust me right up until the moment I made my escape. That was my plan—how I was going to pull it off was anybody's guess.

I set my snares, then went back to the cabin and dug out mine and Jenny's cane poles. Holding her hand, we went to the river and set about to do some fishing. Jenny was two steps behind me suddenly, not wanting to be left alone in the house with those men. I gathered worms and baited our hooks, and then we dropped our lines in the water. We were in the shade of the river, and in no time we had a bait of fish on our rope. Mostly they were blue gill, but we had us a couple of catfish too.

About mid-morning, Culpepper came out to the river to see what we were up to. I pulled up my rope, and he was surprised to see a fish, let alone a dozen. He took my string up to the cabin and returned it to us without so much as a word. One thing was certain; Jeremiah Culpepper was not a talkative man, not unless he was behind the pulpit. When he was preaching, he had all sort of things to say about God, the devil and how a man should live. What bothered me was the fact that the preacher didn't have the desire nor did he have the fortitude to live any of what he preached on Sunday mornings.

Now I realize all men are sinners, we are born into sin, but Jeremiah Culpepper seemed to be extra special in his ability to live the opposite of what he preached. It was plain to me; if man couldn't abide by God's laws, what made anyone think he would abide by man-made laws.

The Preacher set out to clean the fish we'd caught and prepare them for lunch. When he called us in to eat, the others had returned from wherever they had been, and we all ate together. One thing was certain as we ate our catch; I began to understand why the preacher was the cook. To paraphrase Ol' Slantface, the preacher could whirl a fry pan.

I didn't understand the preacher's hatred for me at first, but over the next few days a clear picture began to develop in my mind. I knew who he was. I suspected he knew better than to associate with such mischievous characters, yet he seemed to be one of them. He had acted one way in front of his church-going congregation, of which I was a part, and here he was engaged in another type of behavior altogether away from church. If I ever showed up at his church again, I knew I would be in trouble if I opened my mouth. Unexpectedly, the thought crossed my mind that he would see to it I never again went to his church. The fact is, I'd never seen him light a cigar until the day I saw him standing in the doorway of our cabin. The way I understood things, I was learning too much about the Black Creek gun-toting Preacher for my own good.

How could anyone wear any two such different masks and not get confused with his real identity? As these difficult questions unveiled themselves to me, I no longer considered Jeremiah Culpepper a real preacher. He might hold a license of some sort, and he might have been ordained sometime in his past, but the man was now one hundred percent "Pure De' Villain." He was not a man who could be trusted. The preacher was a man I believed would shoot someone out of pure meanness. I couldn't prove my suspicions, but I sure enough had them.

"Drown them," he'd said, and he'd known us from his own church!

I didn't know it then, but I learned by the end of our association that evil would always attack the innocent or the good. I don't pretend to understand why, but there is no mistaking the fact that it would always be so. Such mayhem had existed since the beginning of time, and there was nothing Dillon Childs could do to change the order of things between God and his nemesis, the Devil himself. Evil could shroud itself in a robe and pulpit; this I learned from the preacher.

Still I begged the question, how could such evil hearted-men clothe themselves in Holy Scripture and get away with it? This I did not understand. Over the next few weeks I began to realize, Jeremiah Culpepper was a man who could preach the gospel truth in church on Sunday morning, saving souls for the Lord, then on the way home beat the living daylights out of me. He could cuss and swear all week long in my presence, but on Sunday morning, act like a saint in front of the entire congregation.

As we waited for the contraband to arrive— "contraband" was the term our cabin guests were calling the orphans from St. Louis—such were the things I learned of Jeremiah Culpepper, and the late days of spring turned to summer.

Uncharacteristically, two Sundays in a row, we had ridden to church with Jeremiah Culpepper, and there we were under his watchful eye all of the time. It was my guess this was the preacher's way of keeping an eye on me and my sister. I had not expected us to be allowed to return to the congregation at Black Creek, but the man had told a lie and he needed our presence in church to back it up.

Culpepper had insisted on the fact that my father had left us children in his capable hands, to care for and watch over until he returned from war. On the ride to church, he would slap me, cuss me and beat me, and then get out of my father's wagon with a smile on his face to greet his parishioners. He made us sit on the front pew, just to ensure he maintained control of us, "young unsupervised heathens" as he often referred to us.

This became what I considered my stay in Hell. Jenny cried a lot during those rides to and from church, and I was forevermore inflamed by the preacher's unjust beatings. At first, I had thought that Ol' Slantface was the most dangerous of the villains; the one I had to watch out for, but as the days dragged on, I realized I had been mistaken. Ol' Slantface was a fair-minded man compared to Jeremiah Culpepper. There was no question in my mind that Jeremiah Culpepper was capable of pure evil. He was no child of God, just an imposter. Why? What did he expect to gain? I became forevermore certain there was a special place in Hell for the likes of the preacher from Black Creek.

I didn't have long to think about my misfortune, though, as boys began to show up from St. Louis two and three at a time. They were housed in the barn and chained like slaves to the wall. This is where Ol' Slantface seemed to take over and direct the day-to-day operations. The cook had been running things up to that point, but as soon as the kids started arriving, Old Scratch took over. The men who brought them in would stay and in no time we had a cabin full of sidewinders.

Brad Lee was the first man to show up and it was easier for folks to call him Bradley. I guessed him to be about thirty-five and rough as a cob. The observation was no second guess on my part. He never took a bath or brushed his teeth and as such, the others made him sleep outside because his breath stunk so bad, not just his breath, all of him. He brought in two boys when he came and promptly shackled them to the wall in our barn. Fact is, his only place to rest was in the barn with the horses if he wanted a roof over his head. Most times he just pitched his blanket under a tree somewhere.

I was ordered to stay out of the barn from that point on, I guess because they didn't want me talking to the boys. Not wanting to endanger my own situation, I did as I was told. I took advantage of the situation and spent more time with Jenny, reassuring her that everything would be all right, while I had no earthly idea as to the truth in matters. I was counting on a verse my father always quoted from the Bible at this point, "Go thy way and as thou hast believed, so be it unto thee." It wasn't much, but it gave me a smattering of hope.

I didn't understand it then, but I was living by faith. The faith that everything would be all right for Dillon Childs, the faith that God had his hand on my life, simple naïve faith, the faith of a child. I couldn't explain why I believed such a thing, but I did. There simply wasn't anything else I could allow myself to believe. The alternatives were too gruesome to come to grips with.

I had no way of knowing if we'd be all right, but I didn't want Jenny worrying about what was going to happen to us. I was doing enough worrying for the both of us. Jenny needed a woman around, and I had no idea where or how to arrange such a thing. I wanted her to have the best teacher she could get, but for now all I could do was pray in the dark. I did a double share of that every night while those men occupied our cabin. I had no idea if such a thing would work or not, but I had to try. Pa always said, "If you can't do anything else, you can pray."

The second man to arrive was Daniel Potts, and he brought three more hostages with him. Danny Potts was Brad Lee's opposite. He always shaved of a morning, sprinkled on some Acme aftershave or cologne, and washed up in the horse trough real good before breakfast. He dressed well in a pin stripe broadcloth suit which was black, and wore a bolo tie. He wore French style boots and kept them polished. He wore a holster, but not so a man could see. It was what he called a shoulder holster. This made Danny Potts a very dangerous man, a man who warranted keeping an eye on the best I could tell. I saw him practice getting his gun into action, and he was mighty quick at lifting it from inside his coat. Then I remembered my unsettling dreams, and wondered if I wouldn't someday mimic him in some fashion.

When the next man arrived, Clayton and Clifton pulled up stakes and headed for the Gateway city. I didn't know what for, but it didn't stop me from thinking they were going after their own charges. I was certain that when they returned, they would have boys to chain up.

Oral Dalton brought in three more and fastened them to the barn wall like animals, while I took Jenny upstairs so she couldn't see any of what was going on. It was bad enough that I had to see. I sat there with her for a little bit until my name was yelled up the stairs. I told her to stay in bed and I went down. Promptly I was ordered to help Jeremiah get something ready to eat. This meant I had to start by bringing in more wood for the stove.

The following morning was Sunday, so on our next trip to church I saw my chance to get Jenny to safety and cornered Mrs. Danbury. She was a middle-aged woman who had raised her children to adulthood, and I got a chance to speak to her so I took it, although Culpepper didn't want me speaking with anyone.

"Ma'am, my sister and I are all alone, and I would sure take it as a favor if you could take her in for a little while. I can come and see her regular like, but she needs a woman around to teach her proper things for a girl. I got no way to care for her," and then I felt the hand squeezing my shoulder. It was the preacher!

"Brother Culpepper, I know you are watching out for these youngsters, but I think young Dillon here may be correct. I shall let Jenny stay with me until such a time as things are on a better footing for the Childs family."

"Mrs. Danbury, I am quite capable of judging what the children may or may not need. Their father left them in my care, and I shall keep them in my care."

"The boy wants his sister to have a female to care for her, and I agree." Taking Jenny's hand, Mrs. Danbury did an about-face and headed for her carriage. I smiled inside. I marveled at the lady's ability to put the preacher in his place. I wondered, could I, Dillon Childs, ever command such a presence? I felt the hand on my shoulder squeeze much too hard, purposefully.

"Get in the wagon, boy," and the ugly look in Culpepper's eye told me I was going to get a beating for this one. I would have likely gotten a beating anyway, but this way at least my sister was safe and I could see her every Sunday. Our situation had improved immensely, although I still had to bear the punishment for my actions.

I got beat soundly, just like I suspected I would, and when we got back to the cabin I was brought before Ol' Slantface, where I had to explain my actions. I was on shaky ground here, but I did my best to justify my actions to the Slaver.

"Well, Dillon, I's waiting fo' an explanation," the slave trader insisted. He was tapping the table with a quirt as he rocked back and forth on the two back legs of his chair. I could almost feel the sting of it from where I stood.

"Sir, Jenny was frightened and becoming more so every day. She needs the care of a good woman, or she will carry these days with her for the rest of her life. If she was to see too much, she'd be no good to anybody. I'll be a man someday, I can handle this sort of roughhousing. Jenny will never be a man, and I had to get her away from here before her mind got all messed up."

Ol' Slantface studied me for the longest minute of my life. "You see awl dat in what's happnin' here?" Ol' Slantface wanted to know.

"Yes Sir, I do. She needs a normal family setting as much as we can provide for her, and I saw to it that she got one. I don't care what happens to me, but Jenny needs a home with a woman's instruction. Mrs. Danbury will provide for her and care for her like a little girl needs, until the war is over and Pa returns home."

"I's thinks you right, but your actions show me dat you don't trust me. Whyn't you ask me, Dillon? I would have made other arrangements weeks ago," he insisted.

"I'm sorry, sir, but it wasn't you I didn't trust," I said, staring across the room at Culpepper.

"I's see. Culpepper, de boy has a point. You've wanted to be rid o'dem both since we got here," he accused. "I's tell you sump'm else, I's don't like seeing my mer..., I don't like seeing the boy whipped. If'n you lay hands on him again I's kills you," Ol' Slantface promised. He was staring the preacher right in the eye when he said it, and I noticed his hand was within easy reach of his pistol as he let go of his quirt and waited for the preacher's reaction. That statement surprised me. Maybe I had an ally in Ol' Slantface after all.

For a moment I thought I was going to see the worst thing I had ever seen in my life. The preacher's right hand hovered above his gun-butt for several seconds while he thought. Then suddenly Jeremiah Culpepper looked at me with demons dancing in his eyes, and stormed from the cabin. I got the feeling the preacher was the worst of the bunch, and was only doing as Slantface said in order to get to a point where he could completely betray the man, or maybe kill him. Any direction things went, I knew I was going to have to get tough or die. As for dying, I was too young for such a thing in my own naïve estimation.

"You shore's putting a burr under de preacher's saddle, Dillon. If'n I was you I'd fight shy of him fo' a couple of days. You might live longer," the slaver offered.

"Slantface, can I ask you something?"

At my words, I saw insanity flare in the man's eyes. "What did you call me boy," he leaned across the table, glaring at me, his hand once again gripping the quirt.

I looked up in a panic, realizing my mistake. "I'm sorry sir, I didn't mean it!"

The fire in his eyes revealed something I had not seen in the dark complexion of the slave trader. He held still for a moment, then took out his knife, and I saw the fire in his eyes change to something else. "It's all right, boy. I like de name, though you caught me by surprise," he said, his facial expression calming almost immediately. "Slantface, dat's a name becomes me, don't it, boys?" he asked the other men for their confirmation. They shook their heads but didn't say anything, as if they were afraid to answer.

"Well, I wouldn't have chosen such a name for you, but if you like it?" Brad Lee spoke up.

"I's do like it, as if'n I don't intimidate people enough already."

"So you want us to call you Slantface?" Oral Dalton retorted.

"Ain't dat what you's said Dillon, Slantface?"

I nodded my head sheepishly, hoping he didn't pull his pistol and shoot me dead right where I stood. I was not sure where this conversation was heading, but I had slipped up. I had thought of him as Ol' Slantface so much in my own mind, the name just naturally jumped right through my lips and came into being. It spread itself across that room like the plague, and nothing I could do would put the idea back in the box. The name was out there, and forevermore it would be used to describe the slave trader.

"Then Slantface it is!" he finally yelled. "By gum and by golly, young man, I's feel liberated!"

Well, I just stared at him, because I didn't know what liberated meant. I thought any second he was going to get up from the table and come over to where I was and knock me through the wall for calling him such a name. My own use of the name Slantface when speaking to myself had betrayed me. As things turned out, I had been worried about nothing. In fact, I'd just earned the respect of Ol' Slantface, but I didn't know it at the time, not by a country mile I didn't.

"For years, I have wandered around shamed 'cause of what happened to me; now thanks to Dillon I's a free man again. I just dare someone ta make light of me now. Why's Dillon, I's going ta enjoy havin' you around, young man. Never thought any boy would ever get the better of Lucifer Deal, but you sure done it. Why I never! Danny, pour de boy a glass of dat sweet sassafras tea. He done earned it."

Well, I still didn't know what liberated meant, but I was getting the impression it was something good, if the old slave trader's reaction was any indication. I called him old man, but every grownup to me was an old man or woman, because I was so young. Danny set a mason jar full of tea in front of me, and I took a big swallow. Then I looked at Ol' Slantface, and for the first time he was smiling with his teeth, a real smile, crooked though it was.

Now, before I get too far into my story, let me remind you of something. Ol' Slantface was black as the ace of spades. He was a fairly big man; he was very intimidating as he called it. To look at him, you got the idea this man had been in more than a few fights, and they were not accidental bar room brawls. The man had been in some life-and-death battles and he was still alive, which begged the question, what had happened to the other fellows?

He wore a Reynolds-modified colt .44 which was shinier and bigger than most pistols. Sometimes he wore a holster and sometimes he kept it inside his overalls. His boots were low cut, with a pointed toe made from mule skin. The butt of his pistol was walnut, which matched the color of his leather gun belt. He wore a pair of faded blue overalls with no shirt, and a straw hat. Without the gun or the fancy boots, he could have easily passed as one of the slaves he used to sell on the auction block.

As I lay in my bed later that evening, I heard the crack of a whip, and somebody screamed. I sat straight up in bed and then lay back down. They were bringing in more boys. I wasn't sure why, but these men seemed to prefer working late at night. How many boys did they have in that barn now? Judging by the food Culpepper was delivering to the captives, I had to guess between eight and ten, but now there would be more. There was always someone with them during the day. There had to be, for things like letting them use the bathroom and so on. The kidnapped boys had to be watched closely.

The whip cracked again, and someone moaned. Right then I thanked the Good Lord that I was in my own cabin sleeping in my own bed, but I knew if Jeremiah Culpepper ever got a hold of me, I would be done for. I had to watch my every move, and when they got ready to pull out I was going to have to run, otherwise I would end up like the boys in the barn; I knew that much for certain. I was a witness. These men could never allow me to go free. They would take my money, lock me up and send me away, just like the orphans they were bringing in. As things stood, it was more convenient for them to control me as somewhat of a partner, but once they began to move the boys south, all bets would be off, there was no question. Suddenly I heard some yelling in the woods behind the house, someone fired a shot. I lay back in my bed and trembled with fear.

Someone had just gotten shot, and my bet was, it had to be a boy not much older than me. I can't tell you how afraid I became then. All I know was I started to shake and shiver with a fear such as I had never encountered. To me, that shot meant only one thing. They were willing to kill anyone who didn't bow to their will, little boys included.

I began to cry, trying to keep from making any noise which might be heard by the men occupying our home. Thankfully the men were all outside for the time being. I heard Ol' Slantface yell, "What happened?" and then I covered my head with my pillow, not wanting to hear anything more. How could this be? How could things have gotten this out of hand? I was in my own bed in my own home, yet I knew I would soon be joining the boys in the barn. How in God's name could such a thing be happening to children?

My mind was beginning to wander into obscurity. There seemed to be no hope for Dillon Childs. I was outnumbered and outgunned. I didn't even have a weapon which I could use to defend myself against these evil and vile men. I pulled my pillow tighter over my head and began to pray. I had nothing else. If God didn't intercede, I was going to end up onboard a ship bound for God knows where, or I would be dead. It didn't seem to me that the men downstairs would care one whit which approach they chose. They would sell me right along with the other boys or they would kill me. Neither option seemed palatable in my estimation, but it wasn't as if I had a choice in the matter. I would be manhandled just like the other boys, once I was proven unproductive or untrustworthy.

Chapter 4

I awoke the next morning to a nightmare! I made my bed like mother and father had always said I should, and then I picked my way slowly down the stairs. The men were sitting around the table finishing up their breakfast. There was a feeling of gloom in the room and I didn't want to be among them, so I made my way silently out onto the front porch. As I closed the door behind me, I saw two bodies lying on the porch at the far end, and suddenly my head began to spin. Both were covered in blood and both of them were just boys no older than me. They were dead; having been hunted down like wild animals. As my head began to spin my eyes went black, my knees buckled and I fell back hard against the door. I was out cold.

When I came to, I was once again lying in my bed. How long had I been out? Not long; the men were still downstairs arguing loudly.

"I'm telling you that boy is trouble, Lucifer..."

"I told you ta call me Slantface!" he yelled back.

"All right, all right, Ol' Slantface it is, but that boy knows what we're doing; he's going to run the first chance he gets and then where will we be?" It was the preacher talking.

"Preacher, you wrong. I know dat kid. He won't run. He trusts me and I's trust him till he gib me reason not to. I's let you in on one more thing, I trust young Dillon more dan I trust you."

"Your funeral, but if it was me, I'd bury him with those two on the front porch," Culpepper insisted.

"If anyone here lays a hand on dat boy while I am gone, I'll take care of dem myself," Slantface excoriated. "Better yet, I's take's him wid me. Danny, is de wagon hitched up?"

"It's all ready to go, just like you ordered."

Boots sounded on the stairs and I lay there staring at the ceiling in my room, worried about what was to become of me. "You awake, Dillon," Ol' Slantface asked as he reached the top.

"I'm awake, but I'm scared," I admitted.

"Well get up, you going ta town wid me. I'll not leave you with dis bunch of cutthroats. I want you alive when I get back."

He didn't have to tell me twice, no sir. I unlimbered myself from beneath my blankets and slipped my boots on quickly. Stamping my feet down into them, I grabbed up my shirt and put it on. Then I walked over to where Ol' Slantface was waiting.

"I got's ta go to de Bluff and get supplies, send a wire an' such. You ready ta assist me?"

"Yes Sir," I answered.

"Come then, the company round here starting de stink," he admonished.

We went down the stairs together and out the front door to where the wagon was waiting. I knew we'd be gone for two days, maybe three, because I had made the same trip with my father more than once. It was a full day's travel to Poplar Bluff by wagon, and a full day home. If you spent any time at all shopping, it turned into three days. The shortest we had ever made the trip was two and a half, so I was thankful for the time away from the cabin.

As we drove down the lane, which followed Current River a ways, I was mindful of the peace and serenity of the wooded country about us. From time to time we scared up quail along the side of the road and sometimes bigger game darted across our path. It wasn't uncommon to see a squirrel, a turtle or a snake cross the trail in front of us. The ride was quiet for a long spell and then I broke the silence. "How come the preacher wants to kill me?" I asked.

"Preacher's a jerk," Ol' Slantface imparted. After a moment he continued. "He don't want ta kill you, Dillon, he only want ta convince me dat I's makin' a mistake trusting you. Preacher reckons he some shakes of a bad man, but I's got him beat many times over on dat count. Everything he does is just a put-on to convince his friends he de man ta leave alone."

"Well its working real good on me," I offered up.

"Preacher, he's wanna-be bad man, long way from being one. Why, he's just beginning ta learn de ropes."

"When we get to Poplar Bluff what happens?" I asked.

"I's get us a room and we waits until tomorrow to buy what we need."

While the things Slantface said made good sense, I still wasn't completely sure he was correct in his estimation of the preacher. I was of the opinion he was worse than Ol' Slantface in every department a boy could conjure from here to the grave, but what did I know? Maybe Ol'

Slantface was correct. For the time being, I rode along with my captor and was at peace with my own situation; at least as long as Ol' Slantface was around.

We got into Poplar Bluff late in the evening, and Slantface purchased us a quiet room. The Black Water Hotel wasn't much on fancy doodads, yet offered a comfortable homey type atmosphere. There was a large woodstove in the lobby, which during the winter was used to heat the place, but for now was covered tastefully with springtime potted plants. The dining room was done in dark walnut flooring with dark green wallpaper. The tables were all set with green and tan tablecloths, with an oil burning lamp placed in the center of each one. The curtains on the windows matched the tablecloths, making the downstairs warm and cozy.

We ate supper downstairs in the dining room. As we ate, I noticed the paper someone left lying on the table, and the headline read: PONY EXPRESS UNDER ATTACK! Ol' Slantface noticed where my attention was focused and spoke up.

"Probably another lie, Dillon," he said, and he took another bite.

"A lie, why would anybody lie about an Indian attack?" I wondered out loud.

"I was dere de day dat first boy rode out. I was in St. Joe. Dey had reporters from Paris, London, St. Louis, San Francisco and New York; newspaper men from all over de world was dere, yet dey couldn't say who rode out dat day. Dey was sent half way round de world ta cover a story and den nothing! Nothing but dead silence!"

"I don't get it. What happened?"

"What happened? Why, de boy who rode out dat day was Nat Love, a black orphan who came all de way from St. Louis fo' de job. Dat was three years ago, but I's remember like it was yesterday. De new American Hero could not be allowed. He could not be a little black boy."

"So they didn't write the story?"

"Dey mentioned everything possible but de rider who rode out dat day. Why it was the emptiest most anticipated story in history."

"But why? I don't understand."

"Dillon, you is too young ta know about prejudice. You haven't learned de way yet. Someday when you is older you might, but I's believe if prejudice can be slain by mortal man, you could do it."

"What is prejudice?"

"You will see prejudice someday, you might even see it tomorrow, and when you see's it you'll know," my friend advised me.

Well, I thought on the word as I ate, and somehow there just wasn't any picture in my mind of what he was referring to. I finished supper, then as instructed, I retired upstairs to our room and stepped inside, still trying to grasp the meaning of the word prejudice. Ol' Slantface had informed me he had some business to tend to; that he'd be up within the hour.

At first the hotel desk clerk wouldn't allow my friend to stay in the same room with me, but when the slave trader's pistol lay across the counter pointed right at the clerk, the stern young man changed his mind lickety-split.

Our room had the same dark walnut flooring, but the walls were a light tan panel with a brand tattooed on it every so often. I was unsure what the letters were for, yet I had heard of the art of branding a cow. There were fourteen different brands on the wall; I counted them. A small table sat in the corner with a wash basin, wash cloth and a hand towel. A full pitcher of water sat beside it. The bed was covered in a multi-colored quilt accented in dark green, which had obviously been hand stitched by several very talented ladies. There were mallard ducks on the face of the quilt, which caused me to want to take the blanket home with me. This I couldn't do, but I wanted to.

I pulled the quilt back and got undressed. Easing myself into bed, I began to think through my situation. I could run right now, but where would I go? If I did run, I was sure to be caught, what would happen then? All of the trust I had built so far would be compromised. I remembered what the hotel clerk had said about not renting rooms to black folks, but Ol' Slantface said it was for me so they let him have the room. Somewhere before I realized the fact that I was demonstrably tired, I passed out from the day's worry, and slept like a baby until sunup.

I could tell I'd had company, sometime during the night while I had been so tired I hadn't bothered to look up. When I opened my eyes to look around, the bed was all torn up, and I wasn't that restless a sleeper. Slantface had obviously come in later in the evening and gone to bed, never pulling back the covers, then being the man he was, he'd gotten up with the rooster crow an hour or so earlier. I got dressed and went downstairs to the lobby, where I found him setting up to breakfast.

"Have a seat, Dillon. You might as well git a good breakfast in you."

I did as he suggested, and in no time I was feeling better. I had eggs and ham with biscuits and gravy, some strawberry preserves and apple cider. I hadn't eaten that good my entire life. By the time I finished, I had a whole new outlook on things. There was no way Ol' Slantface was a real mean man, he was just a hard man, and there was a difference in my book. The preacher was mean, no two ways about it. I was beginning to understand there was a difference.

The fact that a black man was traveling with a young white boy attracted more than a few eyes, which had folks wondering what type of arrangement we might be traveling under. I could see the question mark on their faces, but they'd just have to figure things out on their own. I had no intention of filling them in on matters concerning me and Ol' Slantface. After breakfast, we hit the town and began to gather what was needed for the farm.

We loaded the wagon down good amongst wondering eyes and our task took near all day. We had flour, sugar, tobacco, cornmeal, cheese, leather harness to be assembled in a custom fashion later, extra fry pans and a large kettle for cooking over an open flame and much more. A few of the folks asked questions, but my partner told them it was none of their business. By the time we had the wagon loaded, I understood what the word prejudice meant, for I had just witnessed the twisted mindset firsthand.

Once we had everything secure, we parked the entire outfit down at the stable and went back to the hotel for the evening, leaving our purchases with the hostler. That evening when we ate, the hotel dining room was full of curious onlookers. The word had obviously gotten around about a black man traveling with a white boy, causing many folks to come see the show. After I finished eating, Slantface once again told yours truly to go upstairs and he would be up later. I did as instructed, for I had learned a great deal about people in the last twenty-four hours. My kind was not yet ready to share their own liberty and freedom with the black man. Not if what I had seen earlier in the day bore any measure. I had been witness to prejudice first hand, and what scrambled my brain was; how did folks ever figure to live in a good world if they are not willing to give another race the benefit of the doubt? More than once I watched Ol' Slantface pull his knife out and whittle on his fingernails or lay hand on his pistol until he got his way.

The following morning, after double-checking the security of every item in our possession, we headed for home. We traveled slow and careful, for the wagon was overloaded. This was, in my mind, a good time in my life, considering. Slantface and I were becoming good friends, or so I thought. The only other man who had ever stood up for me was my father, and he was not here. Slantface was more of a mentor to me than my own Pa who was off fighting the war, but whatever the reason for our relationship, I was beginning to appreciate the character he presented and the advice my friend gave.

As we turned onto the avenue about two miles south of the cabin, the sun was way off to our west and another day was coming to an end. Just as we cleared the two big walnut trees at the far end of our property, guns opened up and bullets began to fly. Without thinking, I stood to jump from the wagon and took a bullet through my side.

When I hit the ground, I knew I was only a few yards from the river and I dove in, letting the current take me south. Now, I knew the current was a bad thing to be caught in. I had heard many stories of folks drowning in Current River ever since I was knee high to a tadpole. The Current River meandered through the hills of Missouri and emptied out in the bottoms of Arkansas, but I determined immediately that my chances of survival were better with the turbulent current the river offered, than they would be dodging bullets meant to keep me from taking another breath.

Ol' Slantface had done much the same as me, only he had jumped in the other direction landing in the woods just off the roadbed. I had seen him take at least two bullets before he was down on the ground, crawling for cover. In the distance, I could still hear the guns firing. They had used rifles on us in order to cut us down with no warning, hiding behind trees like a bunch of cowards.

I knew my friend Ol' Slantface was savvy, but was he savvy enough to overcome such a terrible situation without any assistance whatsoever? Suddenly the current did a fair job of pulling me under and my thoughts struck home, I had better worry about my own situation if I was going to live.

After thirty minutes in some very swift current, I pulled myself from the river and crawled out onto the river bank. I was getting a cold shiver from being in the water and I had lost a good deal of my precious blood. My head was swimming more than I was. The sun was down now and darkness had enveloped the land. I had a good idea where I was, but there wasn't anyone I could go to for help. There just wasn't anyone, to my knowledge, who lived this far south of our cabin. I backed myself up under an elm tree and took stock of my wound. I was hurt, but how bad I didn't know. The pain seemed unbearable for a young man such as I, but bear the pain I did.

The bullet seemed to be lodged in my side near my lower left rib. I knew if I was to live, I would have to get the bullet removed and quickly. If my wound was left to fester, blood poisoning would set in and I would be done for. I placed my hand over my rib cage and put a little pressure on the open hole so the bleeding would slow. Having jumped into the river like I'd done, the wound never even began to clot or slow the flow of blood. Realizing my mistake, I knew I was in more trouble than I had ever encountered in my life.

What had happened back there? Those men back at the cabin were our friends, or they were supposed to be, if not mine, at least they were companions of Ol' Slantface. This had to be the work of Jeremiah Culpepper. He had wanted me out of the way from the beginning. What difference would it make if he eliminated his partner in the process? He would instantly be a richer man. Suddenly I realized just what type of man I was dealing with; pure evil! The preacher would not stop until I was in my grave and confirmed dead. He would haunt me and hunt me down until he was certain I was stoking an oven somewhere in hell.

I had to move, but first I had to think and plan. There could be no mistakes on my part. The preacher would be coming for me and he would not stop until my body was turned face down in the swamp somewhere. Either that or he lost track of me altogether. How was I to lose the man? I had to be smarter than him, but how does a twelve-year-old boy with a bullet in him outsmart the hunter? A searing pain ripped through my side and I folded over.

Gathering my feet under me, I knew at once where I was headed. Mrs. Danbury's place wasn't but another six or seven miles from here straight to the east. Jenny was there, and Mrs. Danbury could get out all the warning necessary, provided I could live long enough to reach her. The preacher, Jeremiah Culpepper, would be through in this part of the country. I took about ten steps and doubled over right onto my face landing sprawled out on the ground. I had tripped on a fallen tree limb landing hard.

Struggling to get up, I mustered my strength. Holding my left side, I began to walk as fast as my feet would carry me. About a half mile into the woods I heard commotion back along the river and then I heard a hound dog baying! Where in God's name did they get a bloodhound? My heart sank in despair for I knew if the bloodhound was any good at all my unwanted cabin guests would catch me within the hour and I was leaking blood like a stuck pig. Where had they been keeping the animal?

I had to sprout wings, but in my terrified little mind I knew that was not about to happen unless I took my last breath. I began to run then and I didn't know in what direction. I ran holding a finger in the dike which spilled my life's blood. I set myself to the east, but over and over I had to shift direction to go around a pond or a thicket or some other obstruction until I no longer knew what direction I was headed. I was simply running for my life.

That's when I saw the fire through the woods. The dog was getting ever closer, so I ran toward the fire. As I neared the place where a bunch of soldiers were camped,

I saw the string of horses tied off to one side and made a bee-line straight for them. Lifting the reins of the nearest one, I stepped onto a tree stump, slung myself up bareback and took off, with soldier boys yelling at me in the night. A shot rang out behind me, then more yelling. I didn't know if they planned on letting my pursuit have any horses, but my guess was not. They had just lost one and that was one too many. I held on for dear life and got that horse going to the east, and I didn't stop until I knew I had gained my freedom.

Now, falling off a running horse with a bullet lodged in your side is no picnic, and when I hit the ground I understood what pain was. I wrenched into a God awful shape and lay there for a while, out of breath and nearly out of blood. I was along a swamp somewhere on the Mississippi River Delta. Whether I was in Missouri or Arkansas I no longer had any idea. In fact I didn't know much of anything, for I passed out in my delirium.

I don't know how long I lay there moaning, but it was well into the dark of night when I sensed someone was standing over me. So, they had found me anyway, I thought. I was too weak to open my eyes and look, but someone was there, someone who triggered the picture of destruction in my head. Why didn't they just get it over with and put a bullet in my head, I thought to myself.

"Well now son, I don't know who you are, but if I leave you here you'll surely die. I just hope you can make it to where we have to go," I heard someone say.

"Slantface," I mumbled under heavy breathing.

"What did you say?" It was the voice of a stranger.

"Preacher, kidnapping boys," I managed.

"What are you saying?" The man was having trouble understanding me in my delirium.

"Kidnapped, Pa's cabin, Current River," I forced in a whisper.

I realized the man who had found me was not the same man who had been after me to shorten my days here on earth. In what appeared to be short order the fellow had me in a boat and he was rowing. I don't know how long he rowed, but it seemed like an eternity. From time to time, I would wake up and mutter something incoherent about what was actually going on, yet eventually I must have passed out from lack of blood flow to my brain.

Chapter 5

Captain Grimes, the Confederate blockade runner for the south, had spent a good part of the day on the Mississippi River drifting and playing dead in a boat which looked for all the world like it had been sunk in a flood, had somehow been dislodged from its mooring and was now floating downstream as debris. There was still a good bit of dried mud in the bottom of the skiff, and the manner in which the boat had rested on the riverbank when the mud dried left the boat catawampus while drifting downriver, adding to the deception the boat was not being used. Adding his weight to that of the dried mud, along with tree branches strewn about, left the boat appearing inconsequential to anyone who happened to notice the decrepit structure drifting by, sunk to within six inches of its gunwales on one end.

The boat was working so well to get the captain downstream that he fasted all the first day and into the next, letting himself drift right past most of the Yankee fleet between Cairo and New Madrid, until when near Island Number Ten, a snooping Commander for the Union forces on the Mississippi River ordered the boat sunk to allow his men a chance at target practice. The cannonball which destroyed the skiff also punctured holes in the good captain's nerves, and he began to swim for the

Missouri bank on the west side of the big muddy. Almost immediately, the federals opened up with cannon fire from several ironclads, rifle fire, and there must have been other weapons, because he was being bombarded with enough artillery to lay the entire sector to ruin. How they missed him, with that many weapons firing that much ammunition at one little soul, was a miracle which he counted till his dying day.

The captain was quite certain that by the time he reached shore he was going to die—the moment he pulled himself from the water made sense—but while bullets danced all around like a nest of mad hornets stirred from their hive, not one of them found its mark. He kept running, expecting at any moment to feel the sting of a bullet pierce his flesh or a cannonball cut him in twain. Then suddenly he was away. How the Yankees had missed a running target that many times seemed unimaginable, but the captain was evermore grateful for the inaccuracy which seemed to be designed into the weaponry of the Union soldiers who had fired on him that day.

The Confederate Captain needed his breath back, and he stopped momentarily to count his fingers and toes. His wits were A.W.O.L., and the fact that he was still able to breathe in air without sucking it through new air holes seemed no small miracle. He kept looking for blood stains on his clothing as he walked, but was repeatedly disappointed again and again. He was still alive!

He turned north after a few miles and settled into walking. He walked until dark, and countless times the captain thanked the Good Lord for his providential deliverance. He hadn't been praying much lately, and why the Lord saw fit to deliver him from the fire of the Yankee fleet was beyond the captain's ability to understand, but he was quite thankful just the same. This fact, more than anything, solidified in his mind the idea that he was supposed to be running the mail, which is exactly what he had been doing at the time of the assault on his skiff. The fact his carpetbag full of mail now rested somewhere on the bottom of the Mississippi River was regrettable, yet he had been delivered from the hands of the enemy once again at a time when he should have most certainly died.

The captain could not say why he was special; he didn't feel worthy of such attention from God, but as he walked he concluded that although he could not reason out his own existence, God had something else in store for his life; nothing else could explain why he had been protected, spared from such a sinister barrage of gunfire.

He had made his way back to the swamp area of the Missouri Boot Heel, trudging through the liquid forest, when he heard a noise; a faint groan. Unsure of what to think, he held still until he heard the sound once again. Believing he knew the direction from which the noise had emanated, he once again headed east toward the mighty river Mississippi. As the captain moved cautiously and quietly, he came upon a young man who was obviously injured and needed help.

The boy was all of twelve or thirteen. Though he was not a big kid, he had dried blood all over his clothes, leaving the Confederate mail runner unsure as to whether or not he could help the young man. Obviously, the boy had been running from someone or something. The bleeding seemed to be confined to the upper torso of his body, so Captain Grimes knelt down to take a good look at him.

The young man had been shot and had lost a good deal of blood. Fearful he might not be able to save the young man; he picked him up and took him over to a small hammock which rose out of the swamp not too far distant. Laying him under a tree, Grimes began to assess the damage and pulled the young man's shirt off to get a good look. There was a rope lying at the boy's feet, which must have come from the horse he'd been riding, judging from the tracks the captain saw. The horse, however, was long gone.

The boy needed a doctor, and Captain Grimes was no sawbones. The bullet had gone through his upper torso and appeared lodged in his lower rib area. The open hole in front had been stuffed with a piece of cloth torn from the boy's shirt, which was probably the only reason he was still breathing when the captain found him.

He was unconscious and delirious, moaning and thrashing about at times. Captain Grimes had to find a way to hold him still. Putting together a couple of log poles, Grimes tied his hands and arms to them and then tied his feet. In this way, he could not thrash about and tear the wound open further. There was little else the captain could do without operating tools, which he didn't know how to use anyway.

Sitting down under the tree, after covering the boy with his ever-present captain's coat, Grimes began to contemplate the situation. Someone had shot the young man. Now who in these parts was low enough to shoot an innocent young boy? The young man had to have seen or witnessed some crime, or maybe the bullet wound had been an accident of his own doing; but that was unlikely because he had sought refuge in the swamp. No, the young fellow had to be running from someone.

"Preacher," the youngster mumbled.

Several times Grimes had heard him trying to say a word, but he hadn't been able to make out what the boy was saying until now. "Preacher," now what on earth could he mean by that? Did he want a preacher because he knew he was going to die? Surely such a young boy had nothing to confess which would keep him from the pearly gates. What could he possibly mean?

The boy didn't seem to be aware of what was happening, so maybe he was just moaning in some sort of a semi-conscious dream state. It was a cinch he couldn't eat anything for a while, but he would need fresh water, and the captain only had a little to spare. Captain Grimes opened up his canteen and put the tip to his mouth; surprisingly, the boy took a swallow and then laid his head back.

"Preacher, watch out for the preacher," the boy finally brought to the surface.

"What do you mean, boy, a preacher did this to you?"

"Yes, kid...kidnapped us all."

"You mean there are more of you?"

"Twenty boys and more, Pa's cabin, Current River," he struggled to offer more. The captain's instinct was to tell the boy to rest, but Grimes didn't believe the boy was going to make it, so he let him tell him what he could.

"Where's your Pa's cabin, son?"

"Current River Van Buren by the split rail."

He choked then, and seemed to stop breathing; so he was gone, the captain thought, but a moment later his breathing picked up. Still alive, although unconscious.

Grimes wasn't holding out much hope, but if he understood right, someone was kidnapping boys and holding them in a cabin on Current River. If the boy was to be believed and the veteran mail runner had no reason to doubt a dying kid, why would a preacher be kidnapping boys, and where was he getting them? St. Louis! The streets of St. Louis were overrun with orphans showing up because of the war, this Grimes suddenly remembered.

When the war had started, there were only two orphanages in St. Louis, the Mullanphy Orphanage and the St. Louis Protestant Orphan Asylum, neither of which had been able to handle the multiplying orphan population overtaking the Gateway City. Those two orphanages were caring for as many as fifteen hundred little souls when the Civil War broke out; and now the number had ballooned to anybody's guess. The boys he spoke of had to be coming from St. Louis; boys like Mickey and Bobby Louden, two boys who helped Captain Grimes oftentimes get the mail through.

A number of problems developed in the years leading up to the war which multiplied the orphan population for the city of St. Louis. First off, the city suffered from all of the teething troubles associated with being known as the gateway city. Everyone went there before heading west. The city was unmistakably a major inland port and wayfarer station for those traveling up and down the Mississippi and Missouri Rivers.

In the 1850's St. Louis had the fastest growing population of German immigrants in the United States. Add to that a very large influx of Irish, and the city was overpopulated by 1858. When guardians of children became too sick or poverty-stricken to care for their own, they would drop them at an orphanage, and oftentimes they were never heard from again. Whether they died, or just moved on so they could start over, the orphan population in St. Louis suddenly exploded with young immigrant children who spoke little to no English; thus they also had to be taught the English language.

The orphan population began to multiply. Impure water, little to no garbage disposal and the foul stench of sewage did nothing to help matters. It was not unusual for there to be a cholera outbreak in any given year under such horrid conditions.

When the Civil War broke out, a new category was simultaneously added to the city's woes. Orphans created by the war began to show up, and during the war years, no less than sixty-thousand of the little beggars came to the Gateway City; some stayed, some died, some left, but all of them endured the problems of poverty, inhumane living conditions and crime.

The Orphan trains had begun running in 1854 out of New York, creating yet another dynamic. While New York had solved its orphan problem, it had only shifted the problem to St. Louis. When no home was found, a child was often abandoned at the end of the line—and St. Louis was the end of the line.

The captain was looking around, surveying his surroundings just to make sure no one was nigh upon them, when suddenly the boy spoke again. "Slantface," he muttered.

Now what on earth did he mean? Who was Slantface and who was the preacher? Were they one and the same?

The boy needed to rest, so the good captain didn't try to question him further. He was fighting for his life and Grimes was nearly helpless to aid him.

Slantface! Surely he wasn't referring to the outlaw slave trader, Lucifer Deal. Quite simply put, it was rumored Lucifer Deal would sell his own mother into slavery. He cringed at the thought. He had heard of the man in his personal dealings, moving cargo up and down the Mississippi, and what he had heard was no sort of picnic. The man was as mean as men come. If Lucifer Deal was involved somehow, Grimes knew some of what the boy had been through.

Glancing back to the boy, the captain's heart lurched with a sudden pang. Unless this boy got to a doctor soon, he was going to die. How could the river-savvy captain transport him without injuring him more than he already was? He had never felt more helpless in his life. He knew little of first aid, and this boy needed to be cut open. He needed more than the captain could offer. He required a surgeon and he needed one soon.

If the man or men who did this were still looking for the boy, it was not safe for him to remain in the area. The captain had to get him in a boat and across the river somehow. There was the landing at Reelfoot Lake, Tennessee. Reelfoot Lake was formed in the earthquake of 1811...or maybe Grimes could get him on a troop ship if they had a doctor on board, but what he really needed was a skiff of some sort. To leave the boy here was not an option; he would die and Grimes would be digging a grave he didn't want to dig.

Untying the boy's arms and legs from the poles, he built a travois, wrapping his coat around the poles. Once he had the young man on the device, he tied him in place with the little rope he had left and proceeded toward the river. This was not easy going, however, and the mail runner's efforts would have been for naught had his charge been a full-grown man of twice the weight.

Captain Absalom Grimes was an experienced thinker who understood very quickly that he was leaving a trail anyone could follow, but the boy needed medical attention the captain could not provide. In his own mind, the Confederate blockade runner had to get the little fellow to a doctor or die trying, if he ever wanted his conscience to be clear. This was life or death for the little boy, and he would feel single-handedly responsible for the young man's death if he didn't do everything possible to get him to safety. He would feel responsible simply because of his upbringing, if he did not make a valiant effort.

There would be Federal troops all around New Madrid, so going into the Mississippi delta town was not an option he could explore; however, if he could get close enough to the docks he might procure a boat, which was in the end what he needed. If Grimes could get the boy across the river, he had many friends up and down the east bank of the Mississippi. He might even be lucky enough to secure an army surgeon. Remaining on this side of the Mississippi would be a death sentence for the boy. There had to be help on the Tennessee side, but the Federals were all over Missouri, Tennessee and Arkansas, making travel a hazardous profession for anyone who shined with the Spirit of Dixie.

That was the difference, Captain Grimes thought; Southerners were generally happy people, regardless of circumstance, Yankees always seemed to have to put on a happy face in order to hide an underlying grimace.

The traveling was rough going, but Grimes kept his mind focused on what he must do to enlist help for the dying boy. Trudging through the swamps along either side of the Mississippi River was a tough task, even without a small wounded soul to drag along and the task became monumental. The captain had to stop and rest every fifteen or twenty minutes in order to keep the blood circulation in his arms flowing. Late in the day, he left the boy under a tree on dry land, after making sure he was still among the living. Sneaking down to the river, he found a worthy skiff and slipped the boat loose from its mooring, stepped into the flat bottomed boat and then rowed back in the direction from which he had come. It was a good quarter of a mile inland from the river to where he had stashed the boy, but once out of the current the Mississippi commanded the rowing was much easier.

About a mile south of New Madrid as the crow flies, the captain put ashore and went after his charge. The boy was still breathing and seemed to be resting easy, but now the captain was forced to move him once again.

Picking up the travois, Absalom Grimes started for the boat which floated about two hundred yards away. Gasping, he dropped the poles, exhausted. The little rest he had gotten had taken its toll on the captain. The last two hundred yards were quite simply the most painful; yet there was no help, no one he could trust. He simply had to attempt the rescue alone.

Captain Grimes was an experienced Riverboat Pilot on leave because nearly all pilots were secession and did not like the Federal heavy handedness being levied against riverboat pilots. Eventually, the captain managed to reach the skiff and laid the boy down in the bow, wrapping him with his coat. A smaller boat was simply another vessel to command so Captain Grimes made himself at home then shoved off. The mail carrier wasn't sure if he could recognize the entrance to Reelfoot Lake or if the river was high enough to row through, but that was a chance the riverboat pilot from Hannibal would have to take. Had his friend, Mark Twain been present there would be no doubt, for the he knew the inlet to Reelfoot Lake frontward and backward.

When the water was high enough as it usually was this time of year, an inlet opened up from the Mississippi River which flowed directly into Reelfoot Lake. The night was dark and cloudy and gave him good cover, but Grimes knew he needed to get off the Mississippi River as quickly as possible. Being seen by a Yankee Ironclad was not an option, not if he wanted to survive. If he could get the boy to the landing at Reelfoot, then the youngster might have a chance. There would certainly be a doctor somewhere close by.

A few hours later, the skiff pushed into the submerged tree quarter of Reelfoot Lake, where spruce trees grew from the water, old oak trees were submerged along with cypress; tops still showing, still growing as if nothing had happened; only the roots were as far as sixty foot under water. This was the productive part of the lake where the fishermen took most of their catch. Oftentimes they would snag their nets on submerged trees which did not show above the water, tearing them, which meant they had to repair them. If his memory served him correctly, there was a dock to the south where he could land the boat, and maybe if he was lucky find a doctor for the boy.

He had traveled all day in the swamps west of the river, toting the boy, and then he had rowed the rest of the night, turning his arms into worthless ill-natured hunks of flesh. The sun would be coming up shortly and Captain Absalom Grimes was worn slap out. After rowing in the calm for about thirty more minutes, he saw a fishing dock to the south and made for the structure. He was rowing out of sheer willpower now. There were people on the dock, fisherman who made their living in the lake. Now he would have the help the boy so desperately needed. Leaning forward he checked to see if the boy was still alive. He was.

When he eased up to the structure, several local men gathered around to witness the strange boat in their territory. This was a territory as far as the fishermen were concerned, a secreted land which had to be defended daily. When the lake was formed, the land rights for many locals went fifty to one hundred feet under, farms were buried and land disappeared; but men still held deed to their property, and the water in Reelfoot Lake is like no other because of the New Madrid earthquake. Simply put, the water in Reelfoot Lake is owned by someone holding a deed to the property below.

These men took their land rights seriously, and any stranger coming to their dock was scrutinized as he would be nowhere else in the world. The men in this part of Tennessee were feudal men who still disputed the rights of land ownership, even though the land was below water. They were present daily to make sure no one took fish or game from their land, land submerged since the earthquake of 1811.

When Grimes eased up to the dock with the injured boy, their faces turned somber. "What happened, mister?" The man doing the asking was no doubt a pillar in this community, and it wasn't every day a total stranger came rowing up to his fishing dock with a wounded young boy. He wore a fisherman's knee high boots and raincoat along with a matching hat.

"I found this boy in the swamp across the river, but I couldn't take him into town at New Madrid, because I'm wanted by the Union. The young man has been shot and needs a doctor. I don't know his name," the captain added.

"Skip, Irving, get over here and help get this young lad ashore," he called over his shoulder.

Two men stopped folding their nets and rushed to the boat. They could see something was wrong, but were not able to understand what was happening until they actually laid eyes upon the victim.

"Take it easy with him, he's hurt bad," Captain Grimes instructed.

"Get him into my wagon and hitch up the mules. I'll drive him into town," the lead fisherman stated. "You look all in, mister, how about some coffee?"

"Is there a doctor in town?"

"Nearest thing we have to a doctor. This silly war has called our normal doctor to duty elsewhere, Vicksburg I believe, but if anyone can save him, nurse Chapin can do it."

"She any good?" the captain wanted to know.

"She's better'n Doc Benson most of the time," the old fisherman replied. "Get out of the boat and have some coffee. It's hot, and the boys like theirs thick and black. It'll do you a world of good."

"I can't stay. I've got to go after the others," the captain said.

"What others?" Captain Grimes suddenly had the man's undivided attention.

"The boy said someone is kidnapping boys and holding them in a cabin on the Current River. Somebody has got to go after them and try to free them."

"Hold on, mister, you'll not go alone. Get out and get yourself some coffee. This will only take a couple of minutes," the man said, extending his hand. He helped Captain Grimes exit the skiff, and turned. The fisherman went up the dock and spoke with several men while Grimes waited, nursing his woebegone arms, rubbing them with his blistered hands.

Irvine and Skip loaded the young boy into a wagon normally used for transporting fish to market. While Skip grabbed up the mules, three men grabbed up guns and knives, then started down the dock toward the captain, their faces set in anger. One of them had a big cup of coffee in his hands, and thrust it toward Captain Grimes.

"I'm Roland Inman. This is James Lehman and Hamilton Payne," he said, introducing the two men who flanked him. "We'd be obliged if you'd make room for us to ride in your boat. We want a piece of the varmints who did this, and if they are kidnapping children, we're fixing to fetch home some scalps." Stepping down into the boat, the man named Roland took back the coffee, and once Grimes was back in his boat, shoved the hot coffee back into his hands, then the other men stepped in. Two of the newcomers picked up oars and began to row, while Captain Grimes sat up in the bow and sipped his hot cup of coffee with arms he could no longer feel. For better or worse, the captain had just acquired a three man army.

Chapter 6

Grimes took a good look at the three men who had settled into the boat, and knew instantly he wanted them on his side. They carried a look of toughness about them and he was not wishful to irritate them in any way. Roland Inman had used the word scalp, and his delivery was not lost on Captain Grimes. Scalping was a technique used by the Indians out west whenever they killed their enemies, usually white men, but sometimes this practice was used on other tribes. Whether the Indian's had invented the practice of scalping originally or learned the art from the British, there was no denying the fact they were very capable of scalping anyone who got in their way.

"Let's see if we can disrupt their plans," Hamilton was saying.

They settled into the stolen boat, and the captain figured he'd best tell them where and how he had stolen it. Having visions of being accused of theft in front of these men led him to a hasty confession. "I had to swipe this skiff to get here," he admitted.

"If'n you did such a thing to save the boy's life, we don't much care how you came by it," Hamilton Payne said. "We plan on some shooting, anyway," he said, as he rubbed his gun barrel down with an oil cloth. Roland and

James were rowing, and the captain was never more relieved to receive the rest his arms needed so dearly. The cup of coffee felt weightless in his hands while his arms remained numb.

The coffee was good, hot and strong like it should be, and Captain Grimes sipped the brew as he sat back and rested. James Lehman and Roland Inman did the rowing on the first leg of the journey, but even when the boat reached the Mississippi River, they still refused to let him row. Hamilton relieved Inman, and they continued toward the west bank. They put in at a small inlet near the location Grimes had commandeered the boat, and made their way around New Madrid on foot.

By late evening of the first day, the men were maybe one third of the way to their destination. They made camp under a tree in the middle of a long meadow and rested. James went after dinner, and returned with two large rabbits, which he dressed quickly and roasted over the open fire. The rabbits weren't large fare, but the meat settled Grimes' stomach.

"Why don't you carry a gun?" Roland asked.

"I run the mail from St. Louis to our boys in Mississippi. I don't want to be armed in case I am captured."

"You're not running the mail now," Roland accused.

"No, and just as soon as I can get my hands on a weapon, I'll fill them."

"My uncle lives over near the bluff; he'll have just what you need," Roland added.

"How far is it to Poplar Bluff?" Lehman asked.

"About fifty or sixty miles from the river; we'll make it in the next two days," Grimes added.

Just outside of Poplar Bluff two days later, the men came to a small cabin owned by one Ezekiel Inman, and to confirm what Roland had said, the man had his own personal armory of weapons. Grimes borrowed a Remington double derringer which was still in the original box, an Adams .44 self-cocking revolver Model 1851 and a Spencer repeating rifle model 1860. This amazing weapon held seven cartridges, and would fire all seven without reloading.

His companions loaded up on ammunition and guns as well. When they left Ezekiel's cabin the following morning, Grimes was wondering if the Yankees knew what they were going to encounter as they migrated further south. Some folks in the south, like Ezekiel Inman, were ready for whatever came down the pike. If Ezekiel was set upon by the Union he might die, but he was going to take a whole lot of blue bellies with him.

Two days later, the men neared the Current River area due west of Poplar Bluff. They found a unique spot with a large underground spring dumping its water into a cold river known as Big Spring. Here they drank the fresh water and set up a camp hidden on all four sides. From the looks of things, they weren't the first folks to camp at the site. Current River was less than four miles from their current position in the low valley campground, a short distance considering what they were about to do.

The men spread out in search of the cabin which was supposed to be near something called the Split Rail. Having no idea what the Split Rail was, not one of them knew if it was a train track, a saloon or sawmill, so they set about to asking questions of any local folks they happened to meet. About two in the afternoon, James Lehman came back with the first clue.

"The Split Rail is just what it sounds like. There's a fork in the tracks, which allow a train to continue either north or west from here. West is for the railcars which the loggers use. That's the Split Rail."

"How do we find the fork?" Captain Grimes responded.

"It's about four miles farther West and north from where we are now. If we stay near the river, we're bound to find the cabin we're looking for."

"Yes, Sir, and a pack of trouble, if what happened to that boy is any sign," Roland added.

"Look here, Grimes, the three of us are Night Riders. We can handle whatever we find, but you've got to get them boys away from there. You have got to get them to safety as soon as you can."

"You are all what?" The captain asked.

"Night Riders, and there ain't nothing we can't handle. If we find the place, you get them boys out as soon as the shooting starts. Bring them here to Big Springs and we'll be along directly."

"I'm still trying to understand what you mean by Night Riders."

"If you ever cross us, you'll find out fast enough," Payne said.

"I have no intention of doing such a thing," Grimes declared confidently.

"That's good, because we like you, and I sure wouldn't cotton having to make an example out of you," Hamilton Payne grinned.

"Let's see if we can find that cabin and those children," Grimes suggested. "The boy said it was on the east bank of the river, so we can concentrate our efforts there."

Late in the afternoon, they found what they were looking for; a cabin overlooking the river, with a good size barn off to one side. Hamilton Payne scouted around, and determined the place was being watched and guarded by at least seven men. There were five in the cabin, and two standing guard outside. One of them was watching the barn closely; and to make matters worse, they had them a bloodhound.

"If the boys are being held in the barn, we'll have to eliminate the two outside guards first, and then there's the dog," Roland advised.

"What if they're in irons?" Captain Grimes asked. "They might be shackled. They're holding twenty or more boys. You can't hold a boy any more than you can hold a wild dog. They've got to be chained up somehow."

"Surely they are not being treated as slaves," Lehman answered.

"The boy mentioned Slantface. The only man with a slanted face I can think of is the outlaw slave trader named Lucifer Deal, and although I have never met the man, I'll lay odds the fellow is set in his ways."

"You mean he may have those boys secured with chain and ball?" James asked.

"I wouldn't put it past him, not if the boy was correct," Grimes said. "He'd no reason to lie about something like that, not knowing if he is going to live or not."

"Hamilton, do you think you can sneak around back of the barn and have a look-see? We need to know if those boys are chained up. We also need to know if there is anyone in the barn with them. We can't start a fight to get them away from here unless we first set them free."

"Consider it done, but I can't go back in there until the wind changes direction, or I'll alert that bloodhound they have on the front porch."

They waited for almost three hours for the wind to change direction. When it did, Hamilton moved about with the prowess of an Indian stalking his prey. The men watched as he inched forward each time the guards turned their backs. Eventually, he made his way to the barn and disappeared. A few minutes later, his companions saw him reappear. Again he cloaked his movements behind the backs of the men on guard duty, while keeping a separate eye on the dog. When he returned, Captain Grimes realized what he had just learned from Hamilton Payne. You could be exposed in broad daylight right in front of an armed guard, and he would never see you as long as you didn't move. Movement is what drew their attention, not the fact you were there!

"They are chained," Hamilton reported. "What now?"

"I'll have to go in there after dark and free them. How many are there?" Grimes wanted to know.

"I couldn't see them all, but my guess is somewhere between twenty and thirty."

"How were they secured?"

"Looks like regular irons," he said.

"We're going to need a blacksmith for that," Lehman insisted.

"No, we won't. I can free them all once I'm in the barn," said Captain Grimes.

"Now, how in the devil can you do that?" Lehman asked.

"I have my own technique. Most handcuffs are poorly designed, and I have no trouble getting free of them. It'll be easier with them on someone else's arms. I'll have them free thirty minutes after I enter the barn."

"How do you get out of irons without a blacksmith, without making all kinds of noise?" Roland wanted to know.

"I'll be glad to show you sometime, but tonight you're going to be busy handling the guards and the men inside the cabin. You give me thirty minutes to set them free, and then you can open fire on those mongrels. If they make a move before I get the boys out, open fire anyway. Keep them busy until I can get them all free." Captain Grimes was speaking to all three of his gun-toting companions.

"All right, Grimes, thirty minutes after you enter the barn we open fire; or sooner if they make a move," Roland confirmed.

The men waited for night to fall, and then Grimes made his way to the barn. The posted guards out front had switched about an hour before, so Captain Absalom Grimes was extra quiet and careful. Leaning his rifle against the back wall of the barn, he tried the back door. The large double doors appeared to be secured from inside. That could mean a guard was in the barn. Grimes crept to the window and chanced a look inside. He could see nothing. No one stirred, and all was silent in the darkness.

Walking around to the front of the barn, he slipped between the door openings, and was inside while the guards looked the other way, but the hound sprang up, barking his fool head off, attention on the barn. There was no light inside. Grimes couldn't see, so he held very still. If there was a man in the barn, he was lying in wait. Suddenly, the dog quit his barking and all was quiet. Too quiet!

"I'm here to help you boys," he whispered in a low voice. "We've got to be very quiet, or else the guards or that dad-blamed hound dog will hear us and start howling again.

"Mister, we're all chained up," somebody said in the darkness.

"That's the least of our worries," the captain said. "How many of you are there?"

"Twenty-seven," the same voice responded.

"Is there anyone posted inside the barn to watch you?" Grimes needed to know.

"The men in the cabin come out and check on us every hour or two during the night. Otherwise they don't have any eyes in the barn, if that's what you mean."

"It is. What's your name, son?" Grimes asked.

"Duke John."

"All right Duke, I'm going to free you first, and then you make sure I don't miss anyone. I don't want to leave even one of you boys behind," the captain whispered.

Chatter started among them then and the captain snapped at them. "Hush, ya'll are going to spoil the rescue. Now be quiet."

He freed Duke first, who led him to the next boy. "Hold still," the captain said. "This won't hurt at all."

Captain Grimes pried another set of cuffs open and left them hanging on the wall. "Stand where you are as I free you. Don't anyone leave your spot until I'm finished undoing the lot of you."

Only three boys had a ball attached to their ankles; boys who had tried to escape and were considered a high risk for running. The rest of the boys were only handcuffed and chained to the barn wall. Some were attached around the waist, but a few could walk around freely. In twenty minutes, Captain Grimes had them all free from their bonds and set to work on opening the back door. By now his eyes had adjusted to the darkness and he could make out vague shapes, but the night was still dark and overcast.

Suddenly, Grimes felt the door swing free at his touch, and he turned to the boys. "No matter what you hear or what happens, you boys stay with me, do you hear? There's going to be some shooting in a minute, and we have to wait quietly until it starts. Then we'll be traveling in a hurry."

"Yes, Sir," they whispered in unison.

Then, as if the dog had heard the mass whisper, the bloodhound began to bark and howl once again. "All right, let's go. We're not going to be able to wait," Grimes advised.

Suddenly, as if the dog had heard every word it began to howl, barking into the night with a tattletale bellow. The hound was chained to the front porch of the cabin, otherwise it would have spoiled Captain Grimes plans completely.

"Shut up you silly hound dog," one of the men guarding the boys yelled.

Grimes had freed the boys by wedge and lever, forcing a reverse of the same method he generally used for his own escapes from the Yankees. While steel makes for an impenetrable fortress to keep one in, such metal was poorly suited for keeping one's hands and feet secured, because in 1863, a proper latch system had not yet been developed for such restraints. There was the screw-in type, which held better, but those were not in use here; besides, anyone who wanted could simply unscrew them, as Grimes had learned.

The boys followed Captain Grimes into the edge of the woods, making a good deal of noise in the process. The moment they stopped, they heard one of the guards comment, "Them boys sure are awful quiet tonight. We'd better make sure they're all right. Shut up, dog!"

Both men started for the barn. Just as they reached it, two of Grimes' companions opened fire. Roland was waiting for men to come running out of the cabin, which one did, and he immediately took a bullet in his chest. James and Hamilton, as soon as the men at the barn were down, began to pepper the cabin.

The cabin had no back door, and the only two windows were up high, trapping the remaining men inside. Grimes was optimistic having heard the gunfire, but he knew there were still about four to five men inside the cabin. His question was; which one was Slantface and who was the preacher? He voiced his question to the boys as soon as he thought of it.

"Where is this fellow Slantface?" Grimes asked of the boys as the pushed on.

"He's not here. The preacher ambushed him and tried to kill him about a week ago, but he got away," Bud assured him.

"You mean they're not here?"

"No, Sir, the preacher went to make arrangements to ship us south. They lost track of Ol' Slantface in the swamps, and gave up looking for him, but he's been shot. They were certain they hit him. He lost a lot of blood, so they may have killed him anyway."

"What were they planning to do with you boys?"

"Sell us aboard ship as cabin boys."

"Well, we'd better keep moving if you want to go home," Grimes said.

"Some of us are thinking we might go west and take up a riding job."

"You boys are a little young for that, aren't you?"

"Just how old do you have to be to watch cows?" Duke John asked.

"More cowboys; Lord, that's an awful station to place yourself in, don't any full grown men want to be wranglers anymore?"

"They're fighting a war, captain."

"I guess you're right, Duke, I hadn't thought about it."

Chapter 7

Grimes had emptied the barn, and the boys were anxious to get away from their dark and musty prison. It had been a living hell for them, but they had stuck together to get one another through. Only two of them had been buried trying to escape. Now they were marching through the backwoods, trying to keep pace with the captain as they made their way in the direction of Big Springs. In the distance, they could hear sporadic gunfire as the Night Riders continued to blast away at the remaining men holed up back at the cabin. The terrain here was very steep, with almost jungle-like conditions, but Grimes knew the way back.

"If anyone falls behind for any reason, we must all stop until the situation is corrected," Grimes said over his shoulder. "I have the point because I'm armed, but I can't see everything going on behind me. You've got to tell me what's going on."

"We'll be sure and speak up, captain," one of the boys answered.

Absalom Grimes continued through the woods, heading south and east. The fellows who were helping him had some bloodletting to do, and he thought it was best these youngsters weren't around to see what happened to men who kidnapped little boys. Roland,

87

James and Hamilton could handle themselves just fine, but he didn't want these youngsters to witness such brutality. Men were dying tonight, and the best thing was these boys were somewhere else when the final shots signaled for the grim reaper.

The party walked on for about thirty minutes before Grimes got the first complaint that he was moving too fast and everyone couldn't keep up. He held up long enough to make sure he still had all of his charges before continuing on. An hour later, he could feel his skin crawling with seed ticks and knew he was covered with the bloodsucking varmints, but in the dark it was useless to try and remove them.

Seed ticks are a special nuisance. Even in the best of conditions they're hard to see. They'll go directly for anywhere there is an abundance of hair, except on your head, and burrow into your skin right there. This makes them hard to find, or even see with the naked eye, and the crotch area is usually where the majority of the critters migrate to.

Grimes kept on walking, but he knew by morning he was going to be covered with them, but good. Likely, boys this young had never experienced nature's special torture, so he kept his mouth shut and didn't bother to alert them with the idea anything might be wrong. The boys stayed close together and on his heels for the next few hours, then they came to the spot where the men had agreed to make camp. Big Springs was right there within twenty yards, and building a fire would be an easy thing to do with all of the dead, fallen limbs which were lying around. The boys were an abundance of help in such matters, as they all hurried to gather sticks, gathering more than they could possibly use. They made camp in the open meadow near the water, but not too close to the headwaters. Grimes needed to hear if someone were to come upon them in the middle of the night.

The Captain got additional help moving stones into a large circle he had traced out on the ground, and began to drop tree limbs and kindling into the middle of the pit. He then took one of his good match sticks and struck it on a stone. Lighting the fire was easy; controlling all the fresh fuel the boys kept tossing into the fire was another feat altogether. Young boys and some men for that matter can't leave a good fire well enough alone.

"Settle down, boys, we don't need to burn down the entire state of Missouri," Captain Grimes finally advised them.

"Misery is what we call it," one of the boys spoke up.

"Misery," he smiled to himself. "I can think of a few times I've called her that myself, but in two or three days we'll be below the line in Arkansas. There's not a single mosquito in Arkansas, as they say. They all have relatives, and if you happen to kill one of them, the entire family will show up for the funeral; your funeral. So don't anybody to kill a mosquito; they'll carry you away if you draw first blood."

"Are they that bad?" one of the boys pined.

"They're worse. I mean it; I don't want anybody to slap one, or the rest of them will soon devour us. The smell of blood will draw them faster than the smell of a human being. If you don't know the legend, I am quoting a well-known fact in these parts."

The self-assigned Confederate mail runner settled back and listened to the incessant chatter being created by the little fellows. Laying his head back against the tree, he closed his eyes. It seemed the biggest concern the boys had was not running into the preacher, even by accident. Lucifer Deal didn't really bother them too much, not like the preacher did. Grimes began developing the opinion that the preacher was the devil himself, to listen to the boys talk. Then he overheard them as they began to wonder about a missing young lad by the name of Dillon. It seemed he actually owned the cabin the men had been using to hold them hostage, a place to lay over until the proper transportation arrangements were made to get the boys down river to New Orleans. He thought about the boy he had saved.

Dillon; was that the name of the boy he had found shot and left for dead in the New Madrid swamp? The boy had traveled a large distance in order to get away, no doubt by the way of the missing horse. If Ol' Slantface had been shot, where might he be? Where was the preacher? Had the boy been traveling with Slantface at the time of the ambush? It seemed to him, after listening to the boys' chatter, that the preacher was capable of some mighty low-down dirty deeds, yet Ol' Slantface or Lucifer Deal, as the Captain knew him, seemed to stack up just as bad.

Obviously, the two characters had come to some kind of disagreement. After a bit more listening, he determined the boy named Dillon and Ol' Slantface had been together when they were ambushed by the preacher and the men who had been with them in the cabin on the river.

So, where were the two men, Grimes wondered? Lucifer Deal had been dealing in human flesh for years, if Grimes knew anything at all about buying and selling slaves. Suddenly, with the war in full swing, the slave trade had become extinct. The slave auction house in St. Louis was closed down and converted to the Myrtle Street jail, as if the good Captain, who had been captured by the Yankees three times already, needed any proof. His short visits in the prison had been evidence enough, and things would be much the same anywhere he was housed. So, he came to the conclusion Deal, accustomed to buying and selling human flesh was branching out, kidnapping youngsters no one would miss; orphans created by the same war which had cost Mr. Deal his trade!

"Where are all of you from?" Captain Grimes asked, as he opened his eyes and surveyed the boys. They had settled down a good bit now, and were watching the fire.

"We were all taken from St. Louis. The orphanages are so full some of us have to live on the street," Duke John responded.

"All of you are from St. Louis?"

"Yes, Sir," several boys answered together.

"What's going to happen to us now?" A small boy about the age of thirteen posed the question. His clothing, in the firelight, looked excessively worn and tattered from running through the brambles and the briars of Southeast Missouri.

"What's your name, son?" Captain Grimes leaned forward in the firelight to get a better look at the young man.

"Rassie Cohen."

"How old are you?"

"I'm thirteen." He shuffled his bare feet while his hands fidgeted inside his overall pockets.

"What happened to your mother and father?" Captain Grimes had pulled out his pipe and begun to stoke it with fresh tobacco.

"Pa was killed last year, and a Yankee soldier kil't my Ma." This he said with his head bowed. "That's one Yankee won't be bothering nobody else," the boy muttered.

Grimes understood the last comment. The boy had taken care of the Yankee soldier. "I'm sorry. I don't know what's going to happen to you, but I'll do my best to see that you're returned to where you want to be."

"That would be St. Louis. I was doing all right in the Gateway, even if I was living in a barn loft." The boy certainly had his opinion; he wasn't shy.

"Then we'll see to it you get passage back."

"What about Ol' Slantface and the preacher? What's to stop them from kidnapping us again?" Rassie Cohen might only be thirteen, Grimes observed, but he was a good thinker.

"I may have enough connections in St. Louis to keep them from ever showing their faces in the western port again. The folks I know can organize a campaign with wanted posters, which will make them both think twice before setting foot in town."

"What about the men at the cabin, the ones who got us in the first place; they can still get us."

"No, I don't think there will be any of them coming after you," Grimes reflected.

"What do you mean? Those men are the biggest problem we have," Duke John interrupted.

"There won't be any of those men left alive come morning," Captain Grimes explained. The boys eyes widened in sudden realization, the gravity of the situation hitting home. "Now let's get some sleep. We need to have a good night's rest under our belts when the others get here. When those boys back there catch up with us about daylight, we need to be ready to move."

There were no more questions, for the boys were shocked by the fatality of what their rescuers had done. The thought of all seven of those men who had helped to capture them either dying this very moment, or already dead, sobered them considerably. As the quiet took over, they drifted off to sleep one by one and got some well-needed rest.

When the sky began to grey in the east, Grimes opened his eyes and looked over to see his three esteemed companions making breakfast. They had killed a deer on their way back from the cabin.

"It's a good thing we're on the same side in this matter," Roland commented. "We could have slit your throat and you'd never have known what happened."

"I see you killed a deer instead; but in the middle of the night? How in the..." Grimes started to ask.

"We startled a nest of them by accident, and they scared us half to death, so Hamilton here, he shot one out of pure meanness. Besides, we figured these boys would need to eat. The only food we found on the place was being consumed by the men in the cabin. The supply wagon was gone, and so were any real supplies, else we would have brought the wagon with us."

"I see; well, I'm certainly glad we're on the same side. I'm too tired to be much good at lookout," Grimes stated.

"We dug six shallow graves last night and left a note. One real slick fella got away," Roland informed the captain.

"You left a note?"

"We told Ol' Slantface and his partner, that preacher fellow, they weren't welcome in this part of the country anymore, that they'd better find other accommodations. We also told them the boy was still alive, and that's how we knew where to find them."

Roland walked over and handed Captain Grimes a well done piece of venison, so he sat up and began to eat with the boys. The steak wasn't dressed to his liking, but Grimes wasn't about to complain. The meat was tough, just the same, it was good to be eating something. They had a long day of travel ahead. It was then he was reminded of the ticks, for once again he could feel his skin begin to crawl. They were a devil of a nuisance, almost as bad as mosquitoes, maybe worse.

"I'm covered with seed ticks," Grimes said. "The boys probably are too. We need to get the varmints off so nobody gets sick."

"You're just funning me, aren't you, Grimes?" Rowland was hoping for all he was worth that the man before him was joking.

"No, I wish I were. I'm serious as I have ever been. I believe we're all covered and we'll have to get them off.

"Can't it wait? We need to get these boys out of here," Rowland argued.

"If we wait, the boys and I could get very ill, then what? You'll have a bunch of sick folks to care for and no way to care for them." Grimes paused to study the three men. "No, we'd better set up down by the spring and get the blasted things off before we do any more traveling." Grimes sat grinning at Roland as he took another bite of his deer steak.

"Heavens to Betsy, are you kidding me?" The look upon Rowland's face revealed his terror smitten eyes.

"You know one of you fellows has got to play doctor," Grimes smiled through his white teeth and beard as he picked at his teeth with a toothpick.

So began one of the most stressful and funny episodes those men and boys ever encountered in their lives. In no time, there were more than two dozen children stripped naked, plucking ticks from their bodies; one grown man thrown in to boot. For half the first day, they plucked and pulled, and the ringer was, you can't see your own back side and a few other places, so someone else had to inspect what are considered very sensitive areas of the human anatomy; which led to all sorts of irregular outbursts of laughter, until the adults had finally inspected the boys and picked them clean.

Seed ticks! What earthly purpose did God see in creating such a bug? All Grimes could think was; thank God no women were present. At least they had been spared the most awkward of embarrassments and had retained some of their masculine dignity.

There were plenty of boys in this bunch, but the men didn't really know their names, so Grimes began to write them down in a new diary, or cipher book as he called it, believing the best thing to do was document the event as accurately as possible. This was something he had a habit of doing with everything involving the war. He had long ago learned to keep the book wrapped in waterproof parchment, accomplished by rubbing lard on the leather wrapping and then folding it tight before placing it in his lapel.

He took down their names and got their hometown information so he might at least determine their origins. The men believed such information might prove to be helpful in finding a relative to take them in at a later date. Grimes later added their birthdates.

Buddy Woodford's real name was Stanley and his hometown was Tell City, Indiana. There was Rassie Cohen and Ray Ray Dunn, both from the Caruthersville area in southeast Missouri. These two boys were nearly home already, only there was no family to go home to. Joseph M. Whyte was deaf, hailing from Louisville, Kentucky. All the boys referred to him as "Average Joe," but as the men soon learned, this youngster was anything but average. The young man had overcome his handicap in grand fashion and could read lips, use sign language effectively and talk nearly as well as any other normal young man. In fact, you didn't want to engage him in any kind of a card game, not if you were planning to hang onto your money. If Ray Ray hadn't explained to the rescuers that Joe Whyte was deaf, they never would have known.

Oral B. Capps was an eleven-year-old who couldn't sit still to save his own life. He was from the Gatlinburg area in the Tennessee Smokey Mountains. Captain Grimes quizzed the boy about why he had come so far.

"Everybody knows St. Louis is where the whole world hitches up to go west!" Well, you couldn't get any more honest than that. Kids have the uncanny ability to be brutally honest, so adults are advised to be cautious when asking questions.

Grimes had little ammunition to argue with the young man's logic. If the boys could find a future, they could do so in St. Louis; in fact, all the boys would secure their future in the melting pot which had quickly become known as "The Gateway to the West" during the thirties, forties and fifties.

Hiram "Henry" Parker was from Paris, Tennessee. Nelson "Niles" Howell had walked all of the way from Neosho, Missouri to reach St. Louis. Randolph "Randy" Olson was from Boonville, Missouri. Peter Kilwalski hailed from West Plains, Missouri, while Samson "Sam" Endicott had arrived from Travelers Repose, Missouri.

Jasper Newton was a ten-year-old who had traveled in many different forms to reach St. Louis all the way from Hattiesburg, Mississippi. John E. Freeman was from Mt. Vernon, Illinois, while Anderson "Andy" Shipley was from Humboldt, Tennessee. Virgil Morrison had walked from Carroll, Ohio.

Marty McMahan was the one who really stunned the men. Marty was a thirteen-year-old from Athens, Georgia. He had walked, swum, and hitched rides with other travelers to reach St. Louis only three days before being kidnapped by Ol' Slantface. Actually, it wasn't Ol' Slantface who had done the kidnapping, but it amounted to the same thing. None of them had met Slantface until they reached the cabin on the Current River.

Isaac "Ike" Gastineau had arrived from Mayfield, Kentucky. Leroy A. Webb had come to St. Louis from Oxford, Mississippi. Gregory B. Dalton had drifted by boat down river from the Davenport, Iowa area. John L. Rice had come from Corning, Arkansas. Duke John Robinson was from Greene County, Arkansas, and Bobby

Joe Riggins was from New Madrid, Missouri, but there was nothing left for him in New Madrid. Both of his adopted parents had been killed recently and there was no longer anyone to care for him.

Clark M. Alsup was from Mountain View, Missouri, along with Christopher G. Mosier and Marion J. Sims. William "Shad" Swan was from Pilot Knob, Missouri, and Bradley C. Coleman had come from Mount Sterling on the Osage River. The last young man to account for was Ephraim B. Forest, and he had arrived in St. Louis from Owensboro, Kentucky.

After the captain had listed them all, he studied his tally for a short time and he couldn't help but feel sorry for the poor fellows; he still had his parents. Several of them had explained to the captain that they were being called the "Gaslight Boys," because their home was now on the streets of St. Louis, underneath the oil-burning lanterns which lit the roads by night. It was the farrier down on Broadway who'd coined the phrase before the war even got started.

The Knights of the Golden Circle had gone hunting for more food by the time Grimes had finished his list, so he and the boys talked a bit about their plight.

"What's going to become of us?" Oral Capps asked the Confederate Mail Runner for the south.

"I don't know, son, I do know that you all have the ability to do what's right. What becomes of you from here on is largely up to you. Just because you got a lousy send-off in life doesn't mean you have to let the abuse of today determine your future."

"But we didn't ask for this war," Buddy chimed in.

"No one asked for this lousy war, but it's upon us now and the only thing you can do is survive," Captain Grimes advised. "Listen, all of you! No matter what happens from here on, there is one thing for certain I can tell you. Children grow up! One day you'll all be men in your own right. You'll stand tall, and you'll be tough and capable men making your own way in life. Often times, a bad start leads to a wonderful ending. I've seen it happen again and again. Just because you got out of the starting gate on the wrong foot doesn't mean you won't win life's race."

"If we could keep away from low-life varmints like Ol' Slantface and that preacher man, we might have a chance," Henry offered his two cents.

"Some folks in town don't like us," Sam Endicott added.

"If you don't steal and you don't make a general nuisance of yourself, people will give you a fair shake, but under the circumstances I understand how difficult the temptation to steal may be. You've got to do what is right all of the time; otherwise you'll pay for your crimes later in life, even if you get away with them for the time being," Grimes told them. "A bad lot is no excuse for a young man to start stealing. Habits are a hard thing for a man to break later in life, so you have got to take care and not pick up on the bad ones right now."

"I don't believe you, Mister." This young man was none other than Average Joe, the deaf boy who was adept at reading lips.

"There are as many ways to live as there are people, Joe. What you need to understand is; you decide what happens to you, not other people," the captain said. "Others might influence what happens to you for a time, but ultimately you determine your future by how you respond with your character."

"What loony bin did you escape from?" Joe wanted to know. "I haven't been able to decide anything for myself for some time now. The war is causing all kinds of problems for us youngsters, and now we have to endure slave traders who can't trade their own people anymore. Well, they're still trading them, but they have gone underground now that the slave auction has been converted to prisons."

"When you came to St. Louis, did you decide on St. Louis or Louisville?" Grimes offered in return.

"What?"

"Humor me son, St. Louis or Louisville."

"You know darn good and well I picked St. Louis."

"Why?"

"Because everybody comes to St. Louis who wants to go west," Joe said. "I thought if I could find a way west, I could get away from this stupid war and maybe grow up."

"So did someone else make that decision for you, or did you make it?"

"I decided, but I didn't ask to be kidnapped," Joe argued.

"Joe, you're a very smart young man, but here's what you don't seem to understand. As a child, you started making decisions many years before you ever understood how those decisions will affect you, how much and for how long. You chose St. Louis, but St. Louis is a melting pot of honest people, criminals, soldiers on both sides of the war and travelers from all over the world. I submit that you would not have been kidnapped had you chosen differently."

"But there is nothing in Louisville," Joe squealed.

"There might be nothing that you want, but I assure you, had you chosen Cincinnati or to stay in Louisville, you would not be here standing on this spot this very moment. All decisions involve a certain amount of risk, but the greatest risk we face as people is if we do nothing at all. You're trying, that says a lot about who you boys are, and I don't need to know any more for myself."

The Night Riders returned then, having shot another deer. The men cooked and camped for another day before moving on, but move on they did. When they reached the river, they started crossing the boys with the commandeered boat. This took most of the afternoon and part of the evening, but they got finished eventually without incident and made camp in the woods on the east side of the Big Muddy. At the last crossing, they held up to let a Yankee Ironclad coast downstream, but they got across without incident. Grimes pulled the boat up out of the water and covered it for any future use as might be necessary.

Two days later, they had made their way into Reelfoot Village in Obion County, Tennessee. The small community skirting Reelfoot Lake welcomed their men home and put the boys up as if they were heroes coming home from the war. This was no easy task, and every household had at least one, if not two or three boys staying over. They were cared for, and Nurse Chapin saw to it the final ticks were removed. They were bathed and fed well, along with Captain Grimes, who offered much up-to-date information about how the war was progressing for the southerners.

Captain Grimes stopped by several times to visit, but Dillon Childs had entered into a coma, and the nurse who attended him wasn't sure if he would come through his ordeal or not. After three days of good wholesome rest, Grimes said his goodbyes to everyone and headed back by way of the railhead. He needed to get back by St. Louis to prepare his next mail run, for he had lost his last bag of mail in the river when the Yankees blew his skiff out from under him. Fourteen of the boys returned with Captain Grimes on the train, while thirteen of them decided to try their luck at the peaceful pastime of becoming fishermen on Reelfoot Lake, at least for the time being.

Chapter 8

Two days later I woke up. To everyone's amazement, I seemed to have all of my faculties and was very conscious of my situation. Though I was in a strange place, my understanding was complete about what had happened and I wanted to thank the man who had saved me.

"Captain Grimes has departed for St. Louis already, taking a dozen or so of your friends with him," the nurse said.

"Captain Grimes was the man who saved me?"

"Yes, but there were other men who went back with him to retrieve the remaining boys," she offered. "They live here in Reelfoot Village."

"The preacher shot Slantface; he waited in ambush. He tried to kill us both," Dillon said.

"Lucifer Deal may yet be alive. He's not been found by anyone. The preacher is said to have headed for New Orleans."

"No, Ma'am. He's going after the gold!"

"What gold?" the nurse asked.

"A shipment of gold coming down the Natchez Trace, meant to fund the war for the south. He plans to steal all of it and take a ship to California. I overheard him talking with his men in the swamp when he was trying to kill me," Dillon rattled on.

"You stay right there, young man, I'll be right back!"

Well, I didn't want to disappoint her in any way, not to mention I wasn't going anywhere at all, not for a while anyway. That preacher had done a fair to middlin' job of sending me to the Promised Land. He had tried to kill me, and had my sister been with me, she would now be dead or worse.

I was getting mad. My Pa had always said nothing happens unless you get mad or excited about something. Well, mad was good enough for Dillon Childs. I was going to hunt me down a preacher just as fast as I could get my feet back under me. My intent was to read him from the Good Book and make certain he knew what a bullet wound felt like.

My nurse was gone for about thirty minutes before she returned, but when she did, the old man of the village, August Brewer, was with her. He wore a rubber fisherman's cap and raincoat, and rubber boots, although there was no sign of rain that I could tell. I thought this strange until I learned that he handled fish and nets all day. He had a long protruding nose and deep sunk eyes, along with the biggest ears I ever did see.

"Nurse Chapin informs me you know something of a gold shipment fixing to be hijacked."

"Yes, Sir," I replied.

"And this is money which is supposed to be going toward the war effort for the south?" Brewer asked.

"Yes, Sir."

"Tell me everything you know, young man. We have got to try and stop this travesty."

"All I know is, the preacher Jeremiah Culpepper from Black Creek Church over in Missouri is going to try and hijack the shipment as it comes down the Natchez Trace," I explained.

"I see. Is this an army shipment?" the old man wanted to know.

"I don't know, but they said it would be heavily guarded."

"Well, if it's heavily guarded, there probably isn't much the man can do," Brewer said.

"Maybe. But sir, you must remember the same man shot me in cold blood!" I was adamant about my own circumstances.

"That does add an element of cruelty to the matter. I shudder to think what he would do to the soldiers, should they not be properly warned."

"Sir, you must get word to them. Somebody has to before it's too late."

"That may be all we can do, son. Army boys are trained to fight. If they're warned, maybe it will be enough," the old man said.

I lay back in my bed as Nurse Chapin and the old man left my room. They knew everything I knew at that point. I didn't much care if the shipment was for the north or the south, I just didn't want to see Jeremiah Culpepper end up with all that gold, not after what he had done to me. I closed my eyes and rested for a while. When I again opened them, it was morning. I had slept the night through.

Where was Ol' Slantface? I was holding no grudge against the man, for he had treated me decent, and from all I could tell we were rowing in the same boat now, but there had been no word of his whereabouts. I was worried for him. He might be misdirected just a mite concerning the youth he had tried to shanghai; but the evil one, in my estimation, was the preacher man, Jeremiah Culpepper. I knew this now. Ol' Slantface had taken at least two bullets before he hit the ground rolling. If he took any more, I didn't have a chance to see, because I was scrambling for safety myself. He'd run for the woods, while I'd dropped into the river. Current River had saved my bacon.

Here I was, just a kid trying to grow up, and the entire war effort seemed to be a mechanism designed to remove me from the multitude of the living. I was being hounded at every turn. My mother had already gone on; now it seemed Dillon Childs was next in line for the Grim Reaper. Was the dark stalker ever going to let up? What was to happen next? I didn't see any changes any time soon, which meant I could easily be the next in line for the gathering in of the chaff. In fact, as I grew older I would become more susceptible to being drafted by one side or the other, in what I considered a travesty where I could neither control my future or my fate. This revelation did not set well with me at all. Had I known about the Powder Monkeys fighting for the Union or their Orphan brigade, I would have been aware I could be drafted tomorrow; I thank the Lord I didn't.

Nurse Chapin fed me some breakfast that morning, and a bit later two of the boys who had been at the cabin came to visit me—Rassie Cohen and Duke John Robinson. They were very gracious about thanking me for saving them from a fate worse than death. Then we talked about what was going on with the war and what might happen next, as if little boys would have the slightest clue. It didn't take long for me to learn we didn't know much. I was paying the price for not knowing much already. If I could keep my head on my shoulders a little while longer, maybe I could survive this crazy war.

Sherman and Grant had armies in the area, which translated to the fact that no one was safe, not even a patient being nursed back to health. This bothered me to no end. I couldn't get out of bed, I couldn't run and I couldn't hide if I wanted to. If the Yankees decided to shell the small village on the edge of Reelfoot Lake, I was as good as gone.

Three days later, I awoke to find I was sharing my room with another patient. Ol' Slantface! He was in bad shape, but by grit or by crook he'd made it this far. The men of Reelfoot Village wanted to take him out and hang him, but Nurse Chapin wouldn't let the men have their way. She said if they laid a hand on him, she would come hunting them with a sawed-off shotgun. I didn't know if she was bluffing or not, but the fishermen in the village seemed to set store by her words and no one bothered us, not one little bit, but that was after she shoved cartridges into both barrels and cocked both hammers.

A few days later as I was resting, Ol' Slantface woke up and looked at me. "Well, I's be forever pricked in my soul. Of all de people I should find in my room. How'd you git here, my boy?"

"A riverboat pilot named Captain Grimes fetched me; what about you?"

"I's jus stumbled in here in de middle of de night. Nurse Chapin, she know'd me from days gone by and she took me in."

"Some of the menfolk wanted to hang you when they discovered who you were. Nurse Chapin held them off with a double barrel shotgun," I told him.

"Yep, yes sir, I's can see dat. Dillon, soon as we can move, we got's ta go after a gold shipment. We can't let Culpepper git his hands on it," my friend informed me in his gruff one-of-a-kind voice, which forever sounded like a frog was stuck in his throat.

"The men here in the village have already dispatched someone from the town to notify the army of the preacher's ambush," I explained. "I overheard the preacher and his men when they were chasing me, so we sent someone ahead to warn them."

"You don't know," Ol' Slantface stated flatly.

He was staring at me from across the room as if he couldn't believe I didn't know. I just stared back at him for a moment, and then I said, "I don't know what?"

"Captain Homer Childs, your Pa, is de officer in charge of dat shipment. Dat's how come we found out in de first place. When de wire come in ta let you know your Pa would be coming home for a few days, Culpepper intercepted de message an said dat he would deliver it to you. Dey trusted him a' cause dey knew him ta be de preacher at Black Creek and he had been given charge of you youn'ens. He delivered de message all right. He put two and two together and figured your Pa was de man behind de southern gold shipments. He figured ta eliminate his partner and any problems at de same time— dat being you and me. I's been figuring' two and two fo' awhile my own self, an if'n he get dat gold, he'll cause de south ta lose de war. I don't want dat ta happ'n. I's be out o' business permanent."

My mind instantly turned to panic; Pa under the same guns that had almost killed me and Ol' Slantface. I wanted out of bed right then. I struggled to sit upright, but the pain in my side was stabbing me into submission, forcing me to abandon my effort. How long was this bullet wound going to hold me down? I needed to get up. I had to warn my father! Any warning he might receive would not be sufficient to prepare for any plans the preacher had in mind. Jeremiah Culpepper was pure-D-evil and would plan some dastardly way of tricking the company of soldiers into trusting him, especially since my father knew nothing of his bad side. Suddenly it hit me; my father would recognize the man as an old friend and die for having trusted him. I had to get up!

Again I forced myself to rise to a sitting position on the edge of my bed, fighting back the pain which tore at my body. I was breathing heavily when Nurse Chapin walked into the room.

"What are you doing, young man? You lay back down right this minute," she ordered.

"Where are my clothes?" I said, ignoring her banter.

"I'm not telling you until you're ready to leave here, and you're nowhere near ready to leave. Now lay back down."

"I've got to go. I have to warn my Pa about the preacher!"

"You can wait two days. If you don't, you'll tear that wound open again and bleed to death. Now lay down," she said, raising her voice at me.

I did as she said, but I was not happy. When she left the room again, Slantface told me she had done the right thing. If'n you can wait two mo' days we'll go together. Dat preacher has got's ta be stopped. In two days I's think I'll be able ta go with you. We need ta heal some mo', so let's play along fo' now; come Friday morning we'll insist on leaving, deal?"

"I guess so, but time is important. We need to leave now," I countered.

"We's need to I's agree, but we cain't, not in our condition. Let's both git some well-needed rest, den we'll make up fo' lost time on de trail de best we can. I got us money ta buy horses an outfits. We can do dat laying right here."

Well, I looked at him then, and he knew what I was thinking because he added, "Delegate, Dillon, you got's ta learn how ta delegate, son."

I didn't even know what the word delegate meant, but I soon enough found out. Rassie Cohen and Duke John Robinson came to see me when no one else would because Slantface was in the same room with me. They came and I told them we had something for them to do. They looked a fright at first until we explained what was happening. Slantface made sure they knew exactly what we needed and gave them the money to purchase everything. He told them the better they were able to bargain, the more Yankee greenbacks they could keep for themselves.

It wasn't until years later, when life's circumstance turned full circle, that I learned what destiny really meant. Somehow, someway, all three of us boys had managed to become U.S. Marshals out in the territory, but that is quite another story. Every one of our stories was a different translation, yet we had each netted the same results.

Come Friday morning, we had two fresh horses parked outside, saddled up and ready. Nurse Chapin didn't want to let us go, but she understood the urgency of matters and gave us our clothes. We rode out of there in pain, not fresh and rested like we should have, but hurting and doubled over just from the mounting of our steeds. My friend Slantface had taken three bullets that night two weeks ago and I had taken only one, but the one in me was more painful than his three, or so it seemed. I didn't know then how a man could force himself past an immobilizing pain in order to stay in the saddle.

Finally, Slantface knew I would never make it riding on the back of a horse. He pointed us toward what he called the Mississippi and Tennessee Railroad, which ran north and south all the way to New Orleans. We only needed passage to Hazlehurst, where we would head up the Natchez Trace. This old road had been witness to more crime than any road in the United States up until the present, according to my partner. If we didn't hurry up and get there, the Natchez Trace was going to witness one more dastardly act.

We caught the train south from La Grange, Tennessee, and I settled into a bunk where I could lay down and rest. In one day we covered the distance to reach Hazlehurst, a town which bisected the Natchez Trace about forty miles east of Natchez, Mississippi. Ol' Slantface figured my Pa would still be east some distance. I didn't know how he knew, but he was correct.

Leaving out the following morning for Newton Station, we rode in much better fashion than we had the day before. I was amazed at how much difference one day's rest could make. I was no longer riding doubled over. I sat my horse as straight as Ol' Slantface most times and sometimes straighter. I could tell he was beginning to hurt whenever he really started slouching in his saddle, but we rode on. It was a two day ride to Newton Station and there was no sign of the detachment when we arrived.

From Newton Station, we headed toward Meridian, Mississippi, but not before we had a good meal, which my partner paid for. We got some stares in that town, but only because none of the folks had ever seen Ol' Slantface. They had heard of the slave trader Lucifer Deal, but they had never actually met the man. When we rode out, we traveled about two hours before we came upon the site of the ambush. The army wagon was lying on its side, horses were down, and just as dead were the men we found, but I couldn't find Pa. I was in a panic at the thought the preacher may have killed him. I was certain one of the men was from Reelfoot Lake, but I didn't know his name, yet I remembered seeing him there. The pockets of all victims had been gone through and anything of value had been removed.

"Dillon, what's dat over dere?" Ol' Slantface asked, pointing to what looked to be a well-defended position with shell casings everywhere. The site had taken a barrage of gunfire, stripping trees and bushes of their foliage and bark. No doubt there had been a long siege. Somebody had engineered the fight of their life from a fixed position deep in the tree line.

As the two of us slowly walked toward it, I began to involuntarily heave in my gut, although I didn't actually throw up. All the sign I was witnessing pointed to my father. He would not have given up easily. I knew what we were about to find, and the finding of it was going to drop me, take my feet from under me. It was Pa, just as I had suspected. He was dead. I dropped to my knees and fell on top of his bullet-riddled corpse, bawling like a baby.

"Fo'-teen bullet wounds an de last one a gunshot in de head. Dillon, your Pa was one tough army captain if'n dey had ta put a bullet in his brain after being shot thirteen times. Dat bullet ta his head mean he was still breathing." Slantface lit his pipe and walked off a ways. He was thinking now, thinking what the preacher was up to, where he was headed and how we might catch him. He studied the tracks which were sprinkled about, studied the dead men and he began to calculate in his mind.

"It's a good thing dey is a Judgment God, 'cause killing would be too easy for dat prea'cha man."

My friend was right. Killing was too good for the likes of Jeremiah Culpepper. He needed killing, but he needed torturing first.

My partner let me bawl my eyes out while he went about picking up anything which might do us some good. He was studying the site for any clue which would betray the whereabouts of the preacher. I think, if I am not mistaken, Ol' Slantface wanted to kill the preacher worse than I did at that moment. I must have wallowed in self-pity for hours while he secured the area, as he called it. Finally in the end, he had to pull me off Pa, then he went though Pa's pockets. He handed me the few dollars the others had not found while searching the bodies. Then by accident as we were burying the men, I found Pa's written orders which were lying under a nearby tree. They didn't do anything to tell us where the preacher was headed, but they did say where the shipment was to be delivered. Whoever Judge Pierre Rost was, he was minus one gold shipment.

The gold had been on its way to New Orleans, where it could be boarded onto a ship then used to buy supplies from other countries. We placed the bodies in a shallow grave and marked those we could identify. I vowed to come back and get Pa when the war was over, provided I was still alive when the mayhem ended.

We rode back to Newton Station and borrowed a telegraph wire to report the incident to the officer in charge of the brigade who had shipped the gold. The answer was quite unsettling.

"Get that gold back or the war is lost!" was what the entire note said.

No one needed to tell us that. We already suspected what the situation was, but we were not Confederate Army. The general who had given my father his orders sent a detachment to be under the direction of Ol' Slantface and by divine circumstance yours truly; actually I was just along for the ride. Because we knew the preacher on sight, we became the hound dogs. Wherever we said ride, that's where the army detachment went.

Now, I didn't know how to track a coon through a wet corn field, but Ol' Slantface had some experience in that department. More than once he'd had to track down escaped slaves, so as the situation demanded he put his tracking experience to good use. As for me, I stuck to him like a leech because I had me a preacher to kill!

In less than twenty-four hours, we had seventeen men riding with us when we rode out of Newton Station, seventeen of the toughest men the south had to offer. They knew who they were following, and a few of them had bought slaves from my partner in the past. He had a reputation which preceded him, that of being fair-minded, but also of being relentless in the pursuit of his prey. This bit of information was a comfort to me, because

I now had a glimmer of hope. I believed, in my fertile twelve-year-old mind, we'd eventually find the butcher who had killed Pa and even the score. At that moment in time, I had not the first clue what would actually be required to even anything, but I soon enough learned a man or a boy ought to be careful just what he sets out to do. When you set out to kill a man, you'd better be ready to kill him.

I learned from a master then. I learned how to track a man or a horse through swamp and high ground. I learned to track a man by habits and what he was thinking; not just by what I saw on the ground, but how to develop a thought pattern based upon his living habits. We were two weeks catching up with the preacher, but the preacher from Black Creek had made things easy for us. He must have wanted all of that gold for himself, because he was leaving us a trail of dead bodies as he went. We buried each and every one of the men we found, but for some reason, the preacher never turned a shovel after killing a man.

Two weeks we trudged through swamp land; all the time the preacher was doing his best to cover his tracks, yet he was leaving a trail a blind man could follow. Ol' Slantface wasn't having any of it. Every move the preacher made might have slowed us down, but Slantface was a master tracker. He knew how to track a man in his own twisted little mind. When the tracks disappeared, he tracked the man using his habits and traits. Sure enough, we'd come upon his trail again. Like I said, we followed him for two weeks, all the way to New Orleans.

Now, I had been to the French settlement known as St. Louis, but New Orleans was a French settlement with a completely different atmosphere. While there were plenty of soldiers about, they were all wearing grey. Horse soldiers; all the men who rode with us knew what was at hand. The captain who rode with us, known as James Endicott, sent out a dispatch and we boarded a most modern sailing ship for California. We were going around the Horn, whatever that was, horses and all.

Securing passage, we settled in aboard ship and left New Orleans, headed east and south. The weather was hot, muggy and the stench upon our craft reeked of horse manure. I was given the grand opportunity of mucking out their stalls and throwing the dung overboard. This particular ship, *The Crescent*, seemed haunted at times. I mentioned this to Ol' Slantface and he told me men who died aboard ship sometimes haunted a vessel until it sank or was decommissioned. I'm certain this little fact, as he presented it, was intended to comfort me, yet it accomplished quite the opposite in my fertile young mind. I became the most terrified passenger on the boat.

By the time we pulled into Jamaica seven slow days later, for there had been little wind, I was a complete nervous wreck. My own shadow was scaring me, and I was certain beyond a doubt I was within easy reach of the Grim Reaper. Ol' Slantface told me to go walk the stock with the rest of the soldiers assigned to our detail. I was never so happy to get off a ship in my life. My problem was going to be getting me back on.

Jamaica was an island paradise, and I was not wishful to leave such peaceful surroundings, but I also wanted back what was mine, namely my home and family. My mother and father were gone; I could do nothing about this fact, but my sister, she was all I had left and we still had the land and the home place.

When we left Jamaica the following morning, we had an additional passenger on board and he was only eleven-years-old, one year younger than me. His name was O'Queda Yount, and he was a colored boy. He did as he was told and waited on Captain Edward Hawks hand and foot. When he was too slow or slipped up somehow, he took a lashing with a leather strap the captain carried, along with a sword on his three-inch-wide belt. This little item was the cat of nine tails. From the moment I saw the strap in action, I determined I should never experience the wrath of Captain Edward Hawks.

Five days later, we stopped at the island of Grenada to take on supplies and head south. Again I walked the horses with the troops assigned to this duty, and took a liking to a fellow named Private Chip Dodge. We both wanted to stay in the islands because of the peaceful picturesque view which surrounded us. The water was a blue green, and as beautiful as we had ever seen. You could see all the way to the bottom, although it was so deep in places, you could not reach it by swimming. While some of the crew fished, we swam. Then it was back aboard *The Crescent* for the next leg of our journey; but there were problems afoot, problems I had no idea of.

At Grenada, we took on two more passengers, but they were not the kind of folks I wanted anything to do with. Just to look at them scared the dickens out of me. The two men were of a rough lot, not the kind of friends you would bring home for dinner. One was tall and wore a sword on his hip, and the other was short and fat with a pistol in his belt. Both were dirty. I noticed they kept staring at me, but I was of no consequence to them. I had nothing they could steal, but then, I was unaware of how far down the depravity of man could stoop.

From the corner of my eye, I watched and they always seemed to be looking things over where I was sitting in the shadow of Old Slantface. They wanted something, it seemed, but what? I didn't have anything which would be of any use to them, and neither did my partner. They finally moved along the ship's railing to a different place somewhere out of sight, yet I was now certain the two men were up to no good. They had focused too much on us, so I said something to Ol' Slantface.

"Dey probly never saw de likes of me walking about free onboard ship," he said and shrugged it off.

He was probably right, but I was going to keep a watchful eye on them anyway. I had a good intuition, which I'd inherited from my mother, so I wasn't about to ignore the situation.

By now, I was getting used to sleeping in a ship's hammock, but there were times when the waves made any kind of rest impossible. We put in next at Georgetown, just east of Venezuela. I watched the two men as they watched everyone else. I saw nothing from their behavior which should warn me to be on the lookout, yet something about them didn't seem on the up-and-up.

Then I had an idea; they never did anything. They only watched, and mostly they were watching us. Not just me and my partner, but the troops who rode with us. They were looking for something, it seemed, but what? How could I find out what they were up to? I began to catalog everyone on board *The Crescent,* and I came to the conclusion that those two men were the only folks on her who had no purpose. So, I asked myself, why were they here?

In my mind, I began to call them Apple and Dumpling, the short fat one being Dumpling, but I knew they were more dangerous than what I could conjure up about apples and dumplings. I began to watch them, without looking directly at them, to note every movement they made, and I waited.

The days wore on, and we sailed southeastward to Fortaleza, our first port south of the equator. This city lay in a country called Brazil. We had put fifteen hundred miles behind us, and our trip not yet half complete. This was no island, for we had been seeing land to the south the entire week since leaving Grenada or stopping at Georgetown, and still we had not reached the point where we would turn due south, according to my partner.

As the wind stalled, we were days on the open water; and men upon the open water begin to tell stories, stories which meant something. I listened and learned, but then one day, I myself began to talk, for I had my own story to tell. Private Dodge listened to what happened to me, as did many of the other soldiers. With an acute awareness of what was happening, I noticed Ol' Slantface was listening too.

In all fairness, when Private Dodge suggested to Captain James Endicott that Ol' Slantface would bear watching, I was surprised, but I shouldn't have been. Of course, Slantface had heard every word I said, yet he was not new to the ways of men like I was. For this I was thankful, because if I had been a man and told my story like I'd done, he would have been well within his rights to kill me. The fact that he tried to help me save Pa was to his credit. Ol' Slantface was a hard man, but Jeremiah Culpepper was pure-D-evil, and there is a big difference, I explained to Private Dodge.

Things settled down a mite after Ol' Slantface stared down a few tell-tale looks from the troops he was commanding alongside Captain James Endicott, but the men knew better than to test the man or accuse him of anything. Then things loosened up when we docked at Rio de Janeiro. Rio, as the men called it, was the biggest town I ever did see.

Now, I didn't speak the language, but a few of the men did, and they agreed to teach me a few words in Portuguese, so I wouldn't be handicapped whenever I might be traveling below the equator. At Rio, we got a line on the ship the preacher had taken, and we were only a few days behind the *Salvador*. I should have been looking out for Apple and Dumpling, but the telling of my own story had distracted me.

Private Dodge had let me lead the horses down the ramp in order to let them stretch their legs, and suddenly I had a hand over my mouth and I couldn't yell. All I could do was kick, and when Dumpling grabbed my legs, I was carried away in broad daylight with nobody the wiser. I knew I was in trouble; I didn't even speak the language down here, but I had my hope. I had the hope that somebody had seen me being spirited away, and if not that, there would be tracks in the sand, tracks which did not belong to me.

I continued to struggle, but the two men had an inescapable hold on me. Suddenly a yell went up; Private Dodge had spotted me, and then a shot rang out, but the two men held onto me and tossed me into a waiting trunk then closed the lid down tight. With no warning I was blinded by darkness. No light shown through the tightly sealed container. Two more shots rang out, and then I was dropped and shoved onto the back of a waiting wagon I had seen near the trunk.

I was suddenly panic stricken. Those two men had me, for what I had no idea, any guess on my part was nonexistent. I could think of nothing which would explain my current demise. The wagon beneath me was beginning to roll, not just a casual jaunt either. Whoever was driving me was hell-bent for leather. The horses were flying along and I was rolling around in my box like a snowball headed straight for Hell with no chance at all to divert from my unwilling destiny. Apple and Dumpling had caught me with my guard down!

Chapter 9

I rode in the back of the wagon for what seemed like a good hour before we came to a stop. The men—there were three of them now—hauled me down from the wagon and up some stairs. I was scared. I had been taken against my will, and unless Ol' Slantface spoke perfect Portuguese, I was as good as gone. Even if he could speak it fluently, he would have to find me in a city of thousands of foreigners.

I was getting weak and hot from lack of oxygen. If they didn't let me out soon, I would die right here in the dark and no one would know.

We seemed to top a flight of stairs, and then I was thrust into a room. I could hear men talking, but I lay still. I didn't understand their language at all. I had not had the chance to learn a single word. Some high-pitched yelling was going on around me, then I heard a woman's voice. Still, I couldn't understand a word they were saying, but she seemed to be pleading with the men for something. Suddenly there was a click on the outside of the trunk, and the lid opened to reveal a very pretty woman with black hair standing over me. She reached down into the trunk and helped me to sit up. I was too weak from lack of oxygen to do anything else.

Then she yelled at the men and at once they disappeared out the front door of the room. I have no idea what she said, but the saying of it seemed to light a fire under their feet. Then the door was closed behind the tall man I refer to as Apple, and I found myself alone in the room with her. I looked at her and almost choked. She was wearing nothing from her hips up. Her skirt was of a fashion I had never seen before, but it was her completely exposed chest which captured my attention.

I finally distracted myself long enough to look into her eyes, and I knew instantly I was no better off with her than I was with the men who had kidnapped me. She might be a lady, but in my gut I knew she was going to keep vigil over me until I could be disposed of properly. Disposed of? How would they do that?

She spoke directly to me now, but I didn't move. I looked at her and shrugged my shoulders, indicating that I did not understand. Reaching into the trunk, she grabbed me by the front of my shirt and lifted me upright until I was standing. She didn't figure I was going anywhere, so I stepped out of the trunk and watched her.

Walking over to the door, she thrust one lock home and then another. Turning one more screw-type lock, I knew I wasn't going anywhere at all. While I could reach those locks, I would never be allowed to unlock them prior to being overcome. Suddenly, I had the most mischievous inspiration to run for the door and cause a struggle, knowing full well the only one who could stop me was the half-naked woman. As she passed by me headed for the other room I sprinted for the door in the opposite direction. She caught me as I took my third step and tackled me bodily. I landed hard on the floor, but when I rolled over, she pinned me beneath her knees and began to yell in her native Portuguese tongue. About the moment I realized I was stimulated in a strange fashion, she smacked me hard on the face and got up. Obviously I had done something to offend her, something besides running for the door. Sitting down on the trunk I had been delivered in she stared at me for the longest time.

Finally, watching me all the while, she got up and moved slowly over to a large window and took hold of the curtain. She gave the window covering a yank and jerked it down. There was a rope cord which laced through the outer edge like a belt, which she pulled free, never taking her eyes off of me. Walking back to me, she turned me over so I was face down on the floor once again. Straddling me, she forced me flat so that she could bind my hands behind my back. I could have fought her, but I would have lost the battle. I was still too weak from my bullet wound to last long enough to overcome her. Besides, I had accomplished what I wanted. I now had a story none of the boys back home would believe; that is, if I ever lived to see home again.

Once my hands were tied, she helped me to stand and led me over to a chair by the window. As she had pulled the curtain, I could now see what it was like outside, and I knew I was in trouble. I was in some kind of room four to five stories off the ground. Taking a seat in the chair as directed, I looked over the situation in the room. Obviously my assailant lived here.

The thought came to me as I surveyed the room that I would never see home again. Dillon Childs was out of the picture altogether now. Ol' Slantface would not need me for what he was fixing to do, and I was of no interest to anyone down here, but someone wanted me; otherwise I wouldn't have been shanghaied in the first place. Looking at the trunk, I was glad to be out of it. I had the idea if I was put back into it for any reason, I would likely suffocate.

The room was well lit, as it was the middle of the day. Besides the chair I was sitting in, there were four more located along the adjacent window; directly across from me was a long bench. In the middle of the room was my trunk, but behind it was a rectangular shaped table. The walls were a light peach color, and the floor was dark wood. A picture of a sailing ship hung on one wall, while pictures of people adorned the rest of them. A doorway led to another room, but this I assumed would be her sleeping quarters. I could see the end of a made-up bed.

She said something then, but I didn't understand her. I sat still and waited for her to respond. Not understanding the language, I was at a disadvantage. If she could speak English, I might have a chance, but it seemed if she could do that she would have already done so.

I held on as the hours declined into darkness. She lit a single candle so we might have light, but I didn't want to see anymore. Eventually there was a knock on the door, and she went to it, released all of the locks, then slowly swung it open. The knock had been a signal of some kind, first one, then three, then one again. I made a note of this and filed the information away until such a time as I might need to use it myself. I was not planning on staying here. I knew *The Crescent* had likely sailed by now, but I had no intention of living my life in a far-away unknown land, even if the women didn't wear anything above the hip.

A man stepped into the room and spoke to her in a quiet whispering manner and handed her something which was wrapped up. Then my nose smelled it. The man had brought us something to eat. Well, he had brought her something, and I didn't think she would let me starve while she ate her bounty. I almost missed my guess on that count. She ate her fill and folded the flap back over the remainder of whatever it was she had been eating. It was a strange food to me; I had never smelled the like, but I knew food when I saw it, even in a strange land. My heart wilted at the thought she might not feed me, but then she went into the bedroom, brought out a knife and put it to my throat. She spoke again, and although I couldn't understand a lick of what she said, I understood her meaning clearly.

Lowering the knife, she untied my ropes, led me to the chair and pushed me down into it, where I could eat as she had done. Slowly and carefully, I uncovered the food and looked at what was left. She had eaten well and left only a small portion for me, but I wasn't about to complain. Carefully, with my eyes watching her, I ate my first bite since leaving the ship. The food was good fare whatever it was.

As I ate, I looked her over once again. She had braided her long black hair, which changed her overall looks a good deal. She then went to the bedroom and removed her skirt, revealing light green panties, so that she was now even more scantily clad, her feminine figure uncovered completely. This was something I wasn't used to, and I had a hard time being comfortable in the same abode with her. What kind of country was this, anyway?

When she had put the knife to my neck, she had rubbed one of her breasts against me. I'm not sure if it was on purpose or by accident, but my feeling was she had done it on purpose, almost as if she had gotten a kick out of it. The girl was no old lady, she was pretty, but I had my druthers when it came to girls and she just was not my type. Besides, I couldn't understand a word she said.

I finished my food, and she told me to go into the bedroom; this I understood because she was pointing the knife in that direction and ordering me to do something. Slowly I obeyed her, and then she pushed me down onto the bed. This maneuver startled me, because I was unsure just what her intentions might be.

Climbing on top of me, she again flipped me over and tied my hands behind my back. Then she flipped me back over. She waved the knife in my face, said a few words and left the room. I was getting the idea she wanted me to go to sleep, so I did just that. I was tired and exhausted from my ordeal, so I figured to let the men outside fret and wonder and lose some sleep.

When I awoke in the middle of the night, I looked over my shoulder, and she was there behind me. I was bound still, but I could maneuver if I needed to. I worked my bonds loose and then slipped my left hand free. Ever so slowly, I turned over in the bed to get a better look at my unexpected roommate. She was naked from head to toe. I felt the urge to reach out and touch her, but I resisted such an error of thought. I knew if I made contact, I was liable to get a knife in my chest.

I'd never been in the same bed with a beautiful naked woman before, and I would probably not likely be again, but I was certain about one thing; I had to get away from here. I still had no idea why I had been kidnapped, or why I was being held. I gazed upon her untold beauty masked by darkness, yet I withheld my touch and eased myself out of her bed.

I tiptoed over to the front door and stopped in my tracks. Someone was talking on the other side. They were speaking perfect English, and I was the benefactor.

"We must kill him. There's no other way," someone was saying.

"You're too gory for your own good, Bolo. The boy is no trouble. He has no idea why he's been taken; he's in a foreign land and he doesn't speak the language. He'll never try to escape. Angelina will not allow it anyway."

"Angelina. That's another thing altogether. I want her."

"You want her," the other man said incredulously. "That's just great, we've got a kidnapped boy to worry about, and you're breaking out in monkey bites."

"So?"

"So if you don't watch it, you're going to screw this up like you screw everything up."

"Not so," the man protested.

"Yes so, and I'm not going to bail you out this time."

The conversation dried up at that, and I was greeted by silence from then on. I wasn't going anywhere tonight. Those men were guarding the front door and I suspected it was Apple and Dumpling, Dumpling being the one who wanted to kill me. Who were these guys? One was named Bolo, but what of the other one, and who was the third guy, the one who had brought the food?

Cautiously, I eased myself back to the bedroom and into bed. I could think of many ways of inducing torture, because in my mind I had been planning what I would do to the preacher when we caught up with him, but I had never considered sleeping in the same bed with a beautiful naked woman one of them, until now. I tossed and turned the rest of the night, struggling to keep my hands to myself and only fell asleep as the sun was coming up. The thoughts which had tortured me all night were ones which could get a man hung; as for a little boy, I had no idea. I looked at her a few more times in the better light, and it pained me—I was just a child. I fell asleep, exhausted and dreamed of young pretty girls always trying to tie me down.

When I came to my senses, it was nearly noon. The steady sound of rain beating down outside was soothing, and my female friend was nowhere in sight. I got out of bed and went into the other room, looking for her. She was sitting in one of the chairs, looking out the window, watching it rain. I stood in the doorway and took in all of her beauty, and suddenly I didn't care if I was ever found. Her body was a perfect sculpture, accented by the dull gray light entering through the window. She turned and looked at me, but did not move. I had never been around a naked woman before, let alone kidnapped by one. Still, she hadn't dared to put on the first article of clothing this particular day.

She got up and walked over to me. Taking my face in her right hand, she lifted my head upward and looked into my eyes, studying me for a moment, parting her lips seductively as if she wanted to kiss me. She whispered something to me then, and I trembled at her touch. I was scared, but I was also expectant. I could sense her breasts heaving up and down as she breathed only inches away, but I dare not look at them directly for fear of being slapped again.

With no warning, she let go of my face with her hand and walked past me into the bedroom. I turned to watch her walk and realized this woman knew exactly what she was doing to me. Why? To keep me from running away?

The curtain rope lay on the bed where I had left it earlier in the night. I looked at the rope and decided this was my escape. If I couldn't get all the way down, I could at least get to the next floor. The window below would be in exactly the same position as the one above. Somehow I had to get that rope, and do so without her knowledge. No, I needed to get the rope with her full knowledge and trust Trust what, that I was putting it back? That was the angle, but how did I tell her?

I watched as she stepped into her panties and stood erect. I realized then that Rio de Janeiro was hot. Hotter than anywhere I had ever been, and my guess was that she was as dressed as she was going to get for the day. I was scared; I needed to make the right move and I needed to do so now. I stepped over to the bed and took up the rope. I hefted it up and looked at the woman named Angelina. That's right, I knew her name!

My eyes darted to the rope, then back to her, as if I were trying to understand her thoughts. I quivered, not knowing what to do next. How was I supposed to get this woman to understand me? She was looking at me with suspicion in her eye. If I ran to the window in the other room she would overtake me before I could ever get the rope tied off. I turned slowly, trembling as I went. She was watching me with piercing eyes. There was no trust in them, she watched, yet she made no move toward me.

She came around the bed and stood in the doorway, still watching. My nerves were shot as I made my way over to the window and picked up one edge of the curtain which she had yanked from its mooring. Slowly I began to thread the rope back into the eyelets. I quit my trembling and cursed my luck. I was going to have to follow through with my task in order to gain her trust. As I threaded the rope, she mistook my frustration and came over to me, taking both the curtain and the rope from my hands, so I stepped back. I had been threading it incorrectly. She showed me the correct way to put the rope back in, and I proceeded to follow through and threaded the rope all the way back into place. When I was finished, I sat down in the chair by the window, disgusted with myself. I had managed to squander a perfectly good escape plan.

I closed my eyes and laid my head back in the chair. How could I have been so stupid? My opportunity was gone. If I pulled the rope out now, she would know instantly what I was up to. I glanced over my shoulder out the window and down the long building. I was way up high, surrounded by other buildings nearly the same size. City streets went everywhere and were made of cobblestone, much like the wharf in downtown St. Louis. Well, at least the streets weren't mud city.

There was an awning over our window, which led me to look down. Each successive window below had an awning just like the one adorning our window. I wasn't yet a hundred pounds, but I was close. What if I dropped to the awning below? Then what? I looked at the knife lying on the trunk, and I knew. Angelina had returned to the bedroom, where she was doing something. Gaining my advantage, I jumped up, grabbed the knife and dove out the window. I hit the awning below with a thud and started to slide down. Jabbing the knife into the thick material, I cut an opening as I slid, and suddenly I fell through, landing on the next one. I could hear Angelina screaming something up above, but I was gone ten ways from Sunday. I cut the next one open and dropped one more time. I hit the last awning and cut one more open. It was then I hit the ground hard. It stunned me for a moment, but I managed to hang onto the knife.

I heard the clopping of horses as they ran, from where I don't know. Then suddenly, with no warning, I was looking up at Ol' Slantface; he hadn't left me! He stepped down and helped me up onto his horse. Apple and Dumpling came running down the stairs just then, and they ran right into a loaded pistol. Ol' Slantface let them have it. First Dumpling caught one and folded like a sack of potatoes. Apple appeared right behind him, and I could see he was trying to back-paddle his way up the stairs, but it was too late. The revolver fired once again, and he slumped over the rail beside the staircase.

My friend stepped up into the saddle and took a look up to examine the awnings I had traversed, he pulled me up behind him and then we were away. Private Dodge was there and several others, but I was in good hands now. The horses raced down the rain soaked cobblestone streets. I could have sworn they would leave me, but Old Slantface evidently had other ideas. Was the ship gone? Had the men stayed behind for my sake? I cried then, never so happy to see anybody as I was to see Ol' Slantface at that moment. No one could tell of course, because everything was so wet, no one could detect whether I cried tears or if it was rain. I kept my face hidden anyway and held on.

For ten minutes we rode, and then the streets gave way to sand, and I knew we were getting close to the harbor. It had been almost the exact reverse of how the wagon had left the beach the day before, but the ride back had seemed much shorter. Then we were within sight of the ship and the horses slowed.

"You aw'right Dillon?" I heard him ask.

"I'm fine, sir."

"I was fix'n to tear Rio apart. Good thing ya ran when ya did. Ya saved de whole town," he said.

As we sailed, Ol' Slantface promised I could side him, and I got to look at the captain's map every day. At times Captain Endicott joined us. We still had over a thousand miles to go to reach Cape Horn, and I was wishful to be getting my feet back on dry land, but we now had a line on Culpepper; for it had been Culpepper who had paid to have me kidnapped in Rio. Ol' Slantface was not about to let such a shenanigan go unrewarded.

During the next month, we docked in Costa Rica, Buenos Aires, Cape Horn, Santiago, Lima, Ecuador, Acapulco, Santa Margarita and finally San Diego Harbor. When *The Crescent* docked in San Diego, the *Salvador* was right beside us, but the preacher had already taken flight and was nowhere to be found. He had his gold with him, the gold he had killed my father for, but no one could say where he had gone. We hung around Old Town for a few days sniffing for clues when Ol' Slantface came to us in the town square. I was sitting at a picnic table eating a square burrito with O'Queda, Captain Endicott and Private Dodge. My friend, Ol' Slantface had purchased O'Queda's freedom at my request so he was now riding with us. This didn't set well with the captain of *The*

Crescent, but I learned a valuable lesson from the transaction; money talks!

"Caps, de preacher left town already. Dey's only three ways he can go. He didn't leave aboard a ship. De man bought an outfit and two mules. I's can track him anywhere he goes, but he done already high-tailed it," Slantface informed us.

"Private Dodge, saddle up my horse and pass the word to the others. We leave in one hour," Captain Endicott ordered.

"Yes, sir," Private Dodge saluted his captain and was gone.

We were getting close and the preacher knew it. Somehow he knew we were on his tail. We knew this because he'd had me kidnapped at Rio. My kidnapping was the preachers doing, Ol' Slantface was certain of it. I was now thirteen, having had my birthday aboard *The Crescent,* but I was nowhere near a man. I was, however, an orphan. This sad fact presented itself as we left San Diego around noon that day. I had traveled so far since leaving the cabin and burying my father, the thought had not hit me until then, and when it did I began to cry.

One of the soldiers said, "What's the matter with him?"

Ol' Slantface answered, "Leave him be, he'll be aw right," and I cried some more, because I was not so sure as my friend.

Chapter 10

The land in which we rode was barren of anything I considered to be life, although from time to time a rabbit or some other creature would dart out of the bushes and take off running, only to be shot for dinner later in the evening. This practice was amazing to me, but we were, for the most part, going to have to live off of what the land offered from here out.

When the first animal jumped, fourteen guns went off at the same time from the right flank of our column, and the varmint disappeared altogether, rendering the pedigree undistinguishable to the naked eye, but everyone guessed the victim had been a rabbit because of the way it had jumped. There was simply nothing left to eat. Captain James Endicott corrected this practice immediately, assigning only one sharpshooter on each flank to pull a trigger. This saved our precious meat from certain annihilation and saved the company of soldiers on ammunition.

By sundown, we had covered about fifteen miles, and we were beginning to climb the hills east of San Diego. Mountains seemed more like it. We were five thousand feet above sea level when we stopped to make camp that evening, and the night air offered up a chill, even in midsummer. After nearly two months on the ocean I was happy to have my feet back on solid ground, although I had never seen so much sand in one place. Seemed to me we had taken the long way to get here, but Ol' Slantface was like a well-bred raccoon dog; once he was on your trail, he was going to tree the coon.

The following morning, we ate some scraps left over from the night before, had a cup of hot coffee, kicked out the fire and mounted up. We climbed higher and by mid-day were at seven thousand feet, but the tracks of Jeremiah Culpepper were on the ground right in front of us beckoning—come hither. This left me wondering just who the devil was in this game, Ol' Slantface or Jeremiah Culpepper? My money was on Culpepper.

We didn't hesitate to come hither, and that evening we camped on top of a mountain which offered a view for as far as the naked eye could see. I had no idea where we were, but I liked the land we were traveling upon. Game was plentiful; the Confederate Army detail had shot two mule deer and seven rabbits. We sure weren't going to starve anytime soon.

The next day, as we began to mount up after breakfast, Ol' Slantface called me over to the edge of the mountain where we could see forever. He pointed down below and handed me his army-issued field glasses. I could see plainly that a rider was meandering down the side of the mountain on a horse, and he was pulling two pack animals behind: it was the preacher!

Now, I was fixing to run my horse to death down that mountain because I had the man who had killed Pa in sight, but Ol' Slantface grabbed my reins and pulled me up short. "Hold on dere, Dillon. Ya cain't go running down de side of a mountain. You'll git kilt. That hoss'll roll right over de top of ya and if ya think being shot hurt like de dickens, wait'll a horse lands on ya. Now settle down." His gruff voice seemed a mite irritated.

Releasing the reins on my horse, he stepped into the saddle and led us down the mountain. I was wishful to get going, and Ol' Slantface knew it. He blocked my way at every turn. About ten that morning, one of the soldiers behind me had a horse miss a step, and the two of them began to roll. I watched in horror as the horse landed on top of him no less than twenty-three times before his feet came loose from the stirrup. Actually, his entire saddle was ripped from the horse's belly. He was dead and mangled by the time the horse stopped rolling. Both man and horse had landed nearly a quarter-mile below our current position, where the two carcasses came to a complete rest. At the point of rest that was all they were, a carcass to feed the buzzards in the California sky.

Ol' Slantface handed me his field glasses so I could see for myself, and then said, "Dat, Dillon, is why ye must be careful when going down de back side of a mountain. Dere will be times when we have ta git down and walk, but dat is safer dan de alterative," he said.

I didn't figure to argue with him anymore. He had made his point better than he could have had he planned it. I settled into my saddle and paid him mind then. I had already learned a great deal from this man, and I stood a good chance of growing up if I could learn enough.

We picked our way down the back side of the mountain, while Ol' Slantface picked up his field glasses from time to time and checked on Jeremiah Culpepper. He was out there making his way down ahead of us, but at too great a distance for us to take a shot at him. At two in the afternoon, we held up to give the animals a blow and eat something. There was no shortage of meat, although the men were under orders not to shoot again until the captain gave them clearance; the reason being no one else wanted an unplanned roll down the back side of that mountain.

As we rested and ate, the sun ducked behind the high up hills and we were suddenly in the shade. This was a welcome situation at first, but by late evening as we were tracking Culpepper's steps down the mountain, the air cooled off a great deal, and everyone was cold. We halted long enough to dig our coats out of our packs and they helped, but didn't warm us much. It was too dangerous to go on down in the dark, so we made a dry camp, meaning no fire. Not even a cigarette was allowed, for the lighting of it could be seen for miles, and the captain didn't want Culpepper to know we were back here, not yet.

So it was we skipped a hot meal that evening. The feeling was that we had not yet been spotted, and we didn't want to do anything which might tip the preacher off, causing him to run. This seemed like a good idea to me and O'Queda as well. I thought the shooting of our food along the way probably had already warned him, or the horse soldier rolling to his death.

With nothing else to do, I lay back on my saddle and wondered how Jenny was getting along. She was in good hands with Mrs. Danbury. No doubt she was having a much better time of things than her older sibling. How long before I would see her again? Would I ever see her again?

O'Queda was starting to come out of his shell. He had been awful quiet for several days, but now, after seeing how Ol' Slantface was treating both of us, he was gaining some self-confidence. He was sleeping beside me of a night and in the mornings he would wake me before most of the men got up. He always made sure we were ready to go and our horses were properly saddled before the others. He had no intention of becoming a burden to these men, which seemed like a good idea to me, so I began to help him.

According to the map Captain Endicott had purchased in San Diego, we were headed into California's Imperial Valley. Once Culpepper reached the valley, he left out at a good stride, leaving us to navigate at a much slower pace. By the time we hit the valley floor below, he was corn shucked and gone from the mountain. Wherever he was headed, he was in a hurry, which meant we had been seen, according to my de facto guardian Ol' Slantface. The Confederate Army was in agreement, so we put hurry up dispatch under our hooves and made chase.

"He's headed straight for Indian Territory," Captain Endicott said. No one stopped to elaborate, we just kept moving.

O'Queda and I were sitting in the rocking chair; that's what we called it, right behind Ol' Slantface and Captain Endicott, so we listened while the two men discussed our options. "Sure looks like it ta me," my partner quipped.

"Who in God's name is this preacher?" Endicott asked. "He seems to have already been everywhere we're going."

Slantface drew up and halted his mount. "Now, dat's a keen observation, Caps. You is absolutely correct. Le' me think about dis fo' a minute," Slantface said as the captain halted his men.

My next thought was disheartening. I was a slow learner. Why hadn't I picked up on the idea sooner? Why hadn't I realized I was an orphan sooner than I had? What else was I missing? I was disgusted with myself, but only for a minute. Ol' Slantface saw to it I didn't have time to feel sorry for myself. To this day, I am forever grateful to the man for never allowing me to wallow in self-pity for more than the length of time necessary to recognize what I was doing.

"Caps, I believe I know where de preacher is headed. Ya may think I's crazy, but we need ta split up. Pick five to seven good men ta stay with us, de rest can ride back ta San Diego and catch a boat to San Francisco. It's no long shot; I believe we'll all end up dere when dis ride is over."

"San Francisco? You think he's headed for San Francisco?" Captain Endicott posed.

"I know'd he is, I just don't know how much of de money he'll spend fo' he git dere or how long it'll take him ta make de ride. I want de troops in position waiting fo' him when he arrives. If'n we's lucky, we'll catch him fo' he git anywhere near Frisco. We's can stay in touch with your men by wire."

"You're forgetting something. We're riding straight into Indian Territory. We may need every man we have before we get to where we are going."

"If we have to sentence an entire unit to death, let's give a majority of de men a reprieve, Caps. Dey's no sense in every man dying. Besides, de mission is ta recover de gold and return it to de Confederate States of America, not ta die in Indian Territory. If'n de first unit fails and Culpepper makes it ta San Francisco anyway, we's need some men in place ta recover the stolen shipment when he git dere."

"I hadn't thought of things quite in those terms. You should have been an officer in the Army, sir."

"I rather thought I was," Ol' Slantface smiled.

"Lieutenant Trumann, front and center!" Captain Endicott ordered.

The lieutenant trotted his mount to the front and reined in facing the captain. "Make ready for lunch, we have decisions to make. I'll deliver my orders as soon as we are finished eating."

"Yes, Sir," Trumann saluted and turned back to face the men. "Fall out!"

We made a short camp while Captain Endicott and Ol' Slantface discussed their plans in detail. I knew where I was going, because I wasn't going anywhere except with Ol' Slantface. He might be considered a hard man by some, but I was learning from him many things which I believed would aid me later in life. The idea that we might all die, those of us following the preacher, stirred me up a bit; however, if I did cash in my chips on this trip, I was going to be chasing the devil from Black Creek church when it happened.

"The two boys will stay with me," Ol' Slantface said. "Then five of your best men to carry on with; the rest of you can turn back."

"Lieutenant Trumann will ride with you. I don't need him with me, and he's a good man. I'll give you Sergeant Ward, Corporal Keyes, Privates Dodge and Loren, and the rest shall return to San Diego with me." The captain was sure of himself and the men he had picked to do the job. No one second-guessed him or offered any other remedy.

The upshot was, O'Queda and I got to stay with the main party, hot on the preacher's trail, and that was right where I wanted to be.

"I figure ta git after him hard from here on, Caps. You turn back and take de *Crescent* on up de coast or whatever ship is available. If anything changes, I's notify ya by wire immediately. Just lay low and wait fo' us or de preacher ta show up. Ya know what's ta do if'n its de preacher."

"This could take a few months more, my friend."

"I know, but we've no choice. I's try ta shorten de trip as much as possible," Slantface added.

As for me, I was running through my mind one thousand ways to die, yet the one most convincing seemed to be falling off the back side of a mountain. Maybe this was because I had just witnessed such an event, but the other was getting shot. Rattlesnakes never even entered my mind at that point. That's the blessing of being a child. The worst thing that can happen in a child's mind isn't the worst that can happen, it's just the sum of what he has been exposed to.

So it was, six men and two boys rattled their hocks out of there on a hot sweltering day, and from the looks of things, our environment was not going to get cozy. If our direction didn't change, Ol' Slantface said the hottest part of the country lay ahead of us, along with Cahuilla, Yuma and Pima Indians. I was scared while we were on *The Crescent* because of ghost haunts; now I found myself worried about my scalp. To hear the grown men talk, which wasn't often, Indians like the ones we would encounter could move like ghosts; you couldn't see them until they were upon you, and if you had to fight them, it was best to have no hair, meaning there was no scalp for them to remove.

We hadn't been gone more than two days from the other party when Corporal Keyes began to call O'Queda Yount and me "Salt and Pepper." Slantface just laughed the first time he heard the names, and I wasn't privy to what was so funny. I happened to like my name just fine, but this corporal had to go and start some silly routine. Before the sun rose on the next day, everyone in the party knew us as Salt and Pepper, and they made certain to call us by our pet name from then on. O'Queda, he never seemed to mind.

Now, twelve men had turned back to take the boat up the coast, which was some place on up toward Alaska from what I could tell, and right now I was wishing I was with them, ghost haunts and all, because it was growing hotter and more uncomfortable by the hour. O'Queda and I had new sombreros, which Slantface had been kind enough to purchase for us in San Diego, but right now both of them were starting to look a little weathered and dirty. Sweat was ruining them to my way of thinking, and then dust coming up from our horses' hooves was finishing the job.

Our clothes were beginning to develop salt stains from the sweat we emitted, and our canteens were going dry, but we plodded on, following the tracks of the preacher. We were out in the open flats, nearing the Colorado River, when a bullet kicked up dust at our feet. A few moments later we heard the report of the rifle.

"Retreat," Lieutenant Trumann ordered, yet everyone had already turned their horses back the way we had come, heading for a large rock formation a good distance off. We didn't have to run the horses for very long to get out of rifle range, so we slowed up almost immediately and walked our horses to an area up in the rocky clefts overlooking the desert below. We had cover, and we were protected from rifle fire, but we were out of water and there was no shade, not for a while anyway. What we needed protection from was the sun, and we needed water, but the preacher had all of the water, to our dissatisfaction.

Slantface unlimbered his field glasses and began to watch for signs of movement. After a bit, he lowered them and said, "There ain't no way he gonna wait until dark to leave out. Not now that he knows we's on him."

So we waited for a good two or three hours in the heat of the sun before Slantface noticed anything. "What dat look like ta you, Dillon?" Ol' Slantface said as he handed me his field glasses and pointed.

"It looks like the preacher all right, and he's moving east."

"I's not seen anything else down dere moving about, an' I's been a looking. Mount up, Lieutenant," he told Trumann.

We eased back out onto the desert floor, knowing our horses were in bad shape, and we slowly made our way to the river. At this point we had little to eat, and we had to share what little there was left. I had me a cup of hot coffee on the banks of the Colorado River and lay back against my saddle on the river bank, after taking a nice swim in my clothes to get them cleaned up a little. I didn't care if I was wet. The water felt almighty good after enduring the sweltering heat of the last few days. I was lying on my blanket, not directly on the ground, so in this way my clothes stayed somewhat clean. All of this was action which O'Queda and I had decided upon while watching the men around us.

We had cared for our horses first and let them drink a small bit, then we picketed them away from the water and filled our canteens. Firewood was gathered, and we made an easy fire with the one the preacher had left burning. All we had to do was stoke it a bit.

The next day, we didn't even try to go after the preacher, we just let our horses wade out into the water to cool off and roll around in the desert sand and then cool off some more. We waited the entire day and O'Queda and I spent most of it swimming. This was all right with me, but it seemed we were wasting time.

"Dillon, we's catch him soon enough. In two days you'll be thankful we stopped at dis here river for a day off. De horses need rest and so do de men."

He paused for a moment, then added, "Besides, the prea'cha ain't going anywhere at all. They is fifteen hundred miles of nothing but what you see ahead of us. We'll catch him!"

I didn't argue with him; I figured by now the man knew how to track someone, so he also probably knew how to let his prey ride right into trouble it couldn't get out of. This was a comfort as I thought about things. According to Ol' Slantface, the preacher was riding right into hell, a place with no water and even less shade. It was early summer now, and put lightly, the heat in the southwest desert was stifling, yet it was also just beginning.

What amazed me was the fact my partner knew the geography. How did he know there was fifteen hundred miles of desert up ahead? There was only one way in my book—he had been here before. I didn't say anything, but this led me to wonder just what Ol' Slantface had been through in his life.

Through watching his actions and observing his decision making, I came to the conclusion my friend had been here before, when or why I had no idea, but in my mind I was not guessing such a thing, he had been out west. His motions were familiar to the desert savvy, he didn't waste a single one. While the movement in a swamp required a completely different set of tactics, he was familiar with both, swamp or desert. How, how could he know what to do in either instance if he had never been in the desert?

The answer was simple. Ol' Slantface had been in this part of the country before. He knew where he was going, just like the preacher man. I knew if I kept my mouth shut, sooner or later I would get my answer. The obvious question became, just how long had the two men known each other?

Chapter 11

Ol' Slantface was right of course; two days later I was wishing we were back at the river, lounging in the shade of the few trees and bushes growing along its banks. We were now in Indian Territory somewhere between California and Texas. I couldn't even imagine a thousand miles of nothing but heat-baked rocks and sand. The air was even hotter, the wind was non-existent, and the heat stifling. I was watching our front, back and sides for Pima Indians, because from what I'd heard around the campfire, they were as mean as a ticked-off mountain lion. Some folks back east were squawking about making a state called Arizona from the land we now rode upon, but I couldn't imagine why anyone would want to make a state out of nothing.

We continued to trace the tracks of the horse and pack mules the preacher had purchased in San Diego, ever vigilant of another ambush attempt. The question we now had though: how to close the gap between us and the preacher, without getting caught in his trap. Catching the varmint was not the problem. With no mules to slow our trek we had proven we could run him down anytime we wanted. What we needed was a way to overtake him without being gunned down in ambush.

The terrain was fairly wide open, but there were a bevy of places a gunman could lie in wait with his finger just itching on the trigger of a gun. There was a clump of rocks about two hundred yards to the northeast, another to the south about a hundred yards and several more up ahead, any one of which he could be hiding behind. Mountains lay to the north and south, yet the land we crossed was a barren wasteland. No water unless you knew where to find it. Ol' Slantface assured us he knew where and how to find fresh water, but the preacher led us to the first water hole pretty as you please.

We jumped down to fill our canteens and water the horses, but Ol' Slantface held up his hand and hollered, "Hold on. Lest we forget who we's dealing wid, I think we better make sure dis water is still good and not poison."

"What do you mean poison," Lieutenant Trumann challenged.

"Just what I say; de preacher know we's coming right along behind, an' I wouldn't put it past de sidewinder ta do away wid us by means of poison." Kneeling down, Ol' Slantface scooped up a big handful of water and sniffed it. Not quite sure of himself, he touched his tongue to the liquid and then spit it back onto the scorching sand. "Just as I figured, dat old snake-charmer poisoned de only water hole for miles. He knows we got ta have dis water if'n we's going ta follow him."

"Are you sure this water is no good?"

"I's bet your life on it. We cain't follow him directly, he'll poison de next one and de next one until he know for sure he's kilt us. He's probably sitting out dere right now wid field glasses, watching us dis very minute."

"If he is, we can pretend to fill our canteens and take huge drinks of water. A few minutes later, after having but a small bit of the good water that's left in our canteens, we can start heaving like we're getting sick, and vomiting and then roll over and play dead. If he comes out to verify the fact he's killed us, we'll have him cold turkey," Lieutenant Trumann suggested.

"Now dat's de smartest thing I's heard since leaving Mississippi," Ol' Slantface offered. "Did everyone hear that? Tie de horses off good so dey can't git to de water and we'll pretend ta fill our canteens. Dat means we've got to get them down in de water if he's watching, but don't let any of de water get into your canteen or what you do have will be ruined."

We did as instructed and then took a big fake swallow of the good water we still had, and shortly we were in the throes of agony, fake agony that is. I put on one heck of a show, if I might say so myself, but the men had to calm me and O'Queda down because we were carrying the action a little too far. The spirited words from Ol' Slantface calmed us, and suddenly we were all playing possum. Dead to the world, and not a soul could move or speak without the chance of upsetting our ruse. We lay there until it was nearly dark, yet nothing happened, nothing, that is, until just after sundown, when we heard someone approaching.

We now had two buzzards circling up above and no one was moving, least of all me. Ever since leaving the other soldiers I had been uneasy, wanting nothing more than to kill the man who had killed my father. Now, if my guess was right, he was walking right into our trap, and I could extract my justice. No one would hold my actions against me, yet I lay perfectly still, in abject fear for my own life.

At that moment, I began to wonder if I wasn't a coward. I was quaking from head to toe as I lay in wait to ambush the man who had single-handedly destroyed my family.

The footsteps sounded closer now, and I could feel my spine tingling. I was ready to jump out of my own skin when the men sat up as one and pulled their weapons, which had been drawn and held by their sides, in most cases. Sensing the showdown at hand, I sat up myself for want of not missing what I knew had to happen. When I did, I got the surprise of my life. We hadn't baited the preacher at all, but we had managed to unhinge a young Indian brave about my age. He'd gotten his knife out and was about to take a few scalps or steal a horse and show the folks back home how big a brave he was, but instead he was fairly ensnared in our trap.

He slowly lowered his knife as we surrounded him. No longer trembling for my life, I reached out my hand and took his knife, which he relinquished without hostility. We stared at him then; and you know what, I knew exactly what he was thinking. He was afraid we were going to kill him and eat him for supper right there on the spot.

"Well, Captain, now what?" Lieutenant Trumann asked of Slantface.

"Can't turn him loose; we do, he'll go straight home ta his people and tell dem we are here if dey don't know already," Ol' Slantface elaborated.

"We can't leave him here, either," Sergeant Ward protested.

"No, we can't. If'n we take de youth wid us, his tribe will come looking. When dey see he was taken at dis spot, we will den have a hornet's nest on our backside; dey will believe we kidnapped de boy," Slantface imparted.

"There's no way out of this; they will track us now no matter what we do with him. All we can do is use him to our greatest advantage," Lieutenant Trumann offered.

"And what would that be?"

"I don't have the faintest idea," Lieutenant Trumann said.

"Well, neither do I, so where dat leave us?"

"Sir, may I say something?" I still don't know where my opinion came from, but it was there nevertheless.

"Go ahead, can't hurt nothing," Ol' Slantface imparted.

"If no matter what we do, the Indians are going to come, I say we turn him loose and send him home."

"Can you kindly explain dat logic?" Slantface requested.

"If we prove to be reasonable men, maybe when the Indians catch up with us they will be reasonable; maybe they won't even come after us," I said.

"Now, dat's wishful thinking. Dillon, dos Indians will come, and they will be armed," Ol' Slantface imparted.

"Yes, sir, I'll grant you that, but their intent will be based upon how we treat this boy," I argued.

Ol' Slantface just looked at me like he didn't know who I was. I wasn't sure my own self for that matter, not for a moment anyway. I shuffled my feet in the sand, because the longer the silence lasted, the more I could feel the pressure mounting. I had spoken the last word, and now there was an eerie quiet which had settled over our party. The longer the silence lasted, the more I got agitated. The sun must have gotten to me already to think grown men would listen to anything a youngster might say. I wasn't used to men or anyone else considering my words, yet here they were thinking. Slantface looked me over real good, and then he offered up his solution.

"Give de boy back his knife an' turn him loose. Be careful, Dillon. He's still an Indian."

I extended his knife back to him haft first; hesitantly he took it. I then pointed for him to go. I didn't speak any Indian, although I did speak a little Portuguese now. Slowly, realization dawned upon the young Indian, and the boy understood. Cautiously, he backed away. Turning, he started away, but looked back several times, and I wondered what he was thinking.

Looking up, I saw that our buzzard friends had departed with our rising, disappointed, no doubt, that another meal had grown a set of legs. In a few more minutes it was going to be completely dark.

"Saddle up, we's got a long night ride," Slantface ordered.

We still needed a fresh waterhole, for the one we were leaving was contaminated, poisoned by the preacher. If those Indians got their water here, they would surely die. Had Slantface calculated that fact into his decision? Maybe they wouldn't be coming after all, I thought to myself as I stepped into my saddle. We had knelt down to pretend to take on water, so our tracks indicated we had filled our canteens, but we hadn't.

I wondered about the water for several hours while we rode toward the east, and my conclusion was simple; we had to get the preacher before he killed anyone else. He was a mean and vicious man except when he was in his sheep's clothing, holding his Bible out front. That made him even more dangerous as a villain in my book. Using the word of God to deceive the flocks, yet he was not at all deceiving when in his wolf clothing; he was who you expected him to be. The thing was, when he changed faces in front of you, your number was up. He could leave no witnesses. I understood who he was now, and he had to be stopped. It was coming down to him or me.

We wound our way around the protruding rocks with caution born of days in the saddle, yet we plodded on. Night traveling was more to my liking, and we could get a lot closer to the preacher in the dark, was my feeling. No one said a word as we navigated the sand-strewn wilderness, while the night dragged on. How many miles had we covered? Fifteen...twenty...and still no sign of the man. His tracks were evident though, seemingly highlighted by the moonlight upon the otherwise undisturbed desert floor. In the distance mountains rose about us in every direction, yet we never seemed to get any closer to them. Jagged and wicked up-thrusts of stone rose from the ground in the most diverse places, and I wondered how they had come to be.

At one such outcropping of rocks, we turned due south, leaving the tracks of the preacher behind. This baffled me to no end until I remembered how little water I had left. I understood almost immediately as we headed for a waterhole which would not be contaminated by the preacher's poison. We stopped long enough to give the horses our last bit of water and then we rode on, our precious water completely exhausted. Everyone was counting on Ol' Slantface to lead us to a fresh non-poisoned waterhole.

Where we had been slowly climbing, we were now slowly descending, heading due south. The sun inched over the horizon in the east, yet we rode on. No one spoke, for we all knew how dire the situation had become. We had no one to turn to but Ol' Slantface, the only man among us who had ever been in these parts before. Everyone's future depended upon him. Would he remember after all these years? Ten years is a long time and things changed. If we found the water, what then; did we march right back to where we had left off the preacher's trail?

Suddenly the thought occurred to me that I could die out here and no one would ever know, not my sister, not anyone. I would be bleached white bones sticking up from the sand, after the buzzards finished with me, just like a few I'd been seeing along the trail. Who would know what had become of Dillon Childs, who would care? No one!

We were giving our horses a rest of fifteen minutes on the hour every hour, by getting down and leading them. This was the only way we could make it. If we killed the horses, we were dead men, in my case, dead boy, whose life was only beginning. I weighed all of eighty five pounds give or take, but the men I rode with were double that or more. My weight had been a good deal more, prior to taking a bullet from the preacher. Lately I was shaping up to nothing but skin and bones. I wondered if my horse knew the break he was getting. I stopped and patted his jaw.

As the sun rose higher in the sky, there was no escaping the searing heat. We were in the low bottoms between two mountains, riding slow, when we came to what appeared to be the very lowest point from all directions. There were a few shrubs, and one tree or bush which seemed dead to me, but Ol' Slantface informed me otherwise.

"That tree may be thousands of years old, but it's not dead," he informed everyone. Stepping down from his horse, he pulled out a small shovel which he kept tied to his lower saddlebag. Then he walked over and began to dig. The water was two feet down, but the important thing was, we had water, lifesaving water! When the men saw Slantface pitch the first shovelful of wet sand, everyone jumped down from their horses and began to widen the hole.

In about thirty minutes, we had a waterhole big enough to care for us and the horses, but we still wanted to wait for the sediment to fall to the bottom, thus the horses drank first. We had stirred up so much dirt, the water looked like mud, and while that was fine for the horses, we wanted the cleanest water we could acquire for our personal canteens. Ol' Slantface had led us to water. I'd had my doubts there at the end, and so had the others, but now he appeared as if a hero to us all. The way things were shaping up, if we were going to leave this desert alive, we had better hitch our wagons to Ol' Slantface and not let go.

We stayed the night right there at the waterhole. The next morning we topped off our canteens, drank one final time and let the horses drink their fill, then headed northeast, toward a pass in the mountains which Slantface said would be dangerous. For now, the old sidewinder we were chasing seemed to be headed for Santa Fe or Albuquerque, when he should have been heading toward Flagstaff, up in the Arizona highlands. This was quite puzzling for us all. Not that I knew anything, because I surely didn't, but to the men I rode with, this behavior from the preacher was puzzling.

Once in the mountain pass, rather than try to navigate the pass in the dark, we settled down to wait for morning. We were once again shadowing the man's tracks and were certain this was the way he had come. We built a small fire in a hollow of rocks, where it could not be seen directly except from up above.

The events of the last twenty-four hours had let me forget my little Indian friend altogether. Suddenly I remembered him and wondered what had become of the Indians we had expected to follow us. Had they drank the contaminated water and died or were they back there somewhere coming right along? I almost wished they were coming for us, because I could not imagine the pain and agony of death by poison, and those Indians were set for death if they drank the water the preacher had left behind. I shuddered at the thought and drifted off to sleep.

O'Queda and I were beginning to do just about everything together, so I was not surprised when I woke up the next morning to see the boy had plopped his bedroll beside me. I pushed to wake him, only when the blanket threw back, it wasn't him. My Indian friend had found me. I jumped up to take a look about the camp in a complete panic, yet everyone was accounted for, as my commotion had rightfully stirred the rest of our party from their slumber. If the Indian boy was here, where were the warriors? I fully expected an Indian attack at that very moment, but it never came.

"Settle down, Dillon, you look like' you seen a ghost," Ol' Slantface offered.

I just pointed at the Indian. "You don't see anything amiss here?"

"He came in late las-night after you fell asleep. We didn't figure ta wake you just cause de Indian wanted to travel with us. He went ta sleep, we all did. Dat poison water killed many of de boy's people. He came after us, thought we poisoned de waterhole. I s'plained what happened. Now he wants ta scalp the preacher."

Well, I just stared at the Indian then. "He can have the preacher's scalp, but I'm going to kill him myself," I said, looking the boy right in the eyes.

"Dat's between de two of you ta argue out, I's not have fighting in my camp. Do you understand," Slantface imparted firmly.

"Yes, sir," I stated flatly.

"Put on a pot of coffee fo' we hit de trail. I's need a good cup of java while we has de extra water," Slantface ordered.

Private Dodge wasted no time setting the coffee on to boil. The young Indian watched us closely as we did our morning dance around the campfire, following what was becoming a ritual. His eyes widened a few times as we passed around the coffee pot and fried up the last of our salted meat, but otherwise he watched, not saying a word. Lieutenant Trumann was the man what knew sign language and not much at that, but enough to get by. He had gotten a few answers from the boy when he had come into camp the night before, but so far this morning the Indian was not answering back, only watching.

"What did he say last night when he came into camp?" I asked.

"His people drank the water the preacher poisoned, killed several of the warriors in his family, the ones who were coming after us. Now that we've told him it wasn't us, he wants a hand at killing the preacher," Lieutenant Trumann said.

"He'll have to wait his turn," I swore.

"Just what we told him. He figures you for some kind of a heap big warrior because we said you get first dibs. Indians don't understand a word like try; they either do or don't," Trumann imparted.

"Well, he'd better not get in my way," I said.

"You not get in mine," the Indian chimed back.

Our mouths dropped open in surprise. How had he learned to speak English? We saddled up and rode out then, the Indian riding his unshod pony bareback. He was sure enough going to be a bother, for when we rode I had O'Queda on my left and the Indian on my right. I was completely boxed in by other boys, when all I wanted was my own space. Now there were nine of us and a third of our party was children. Ol' Slantface was mumbling under his breath about being a babysitter of little children and Lieutenant Trumann was complaining about lack of food, but we kept following the preacher's tracks right into the mountain pass; O'Queda in front and the Indian in back of me when the trail got narrow.

Chapter 12

As we got up into the mountains, we stayed single file most of the time. It was a narrow rocky game trail, with cliffs rising on both sides for a better part of the morning. No vegetation showed itself, only rocks and sand. After climbing all morning, we finally topped out on a plateau, leaving the narrow confines of the rising canyon walls behind us. I had never seen so much sand and rock in my life, but riding with Ol' Slantface was making up for my lack of education quite well in most departments.

The place we rode now was called Castle Dome, a lonely corner of New Mexico territory unknown to the casual explorer. To get where we were, you had to take aim on purpose. Our ride was not an easy one. The country about was pretty as I had ever seen, but there was danger also. When the Tank Mountains appeared between two peaks according to Slantface, an informed traveler would turn off the old Indian trail and head due south for the Gila River. This is what we did, leaving the preacher to head due east into the upcoming mountainous terrain. Following the river would leave us with no shortage of water. The preacher was on his own, especially if he intended to poison waterholes all the way to Santa Fe.

"Wid de river we's constant water and we be able ta pick up his trail at de bend, if'n I know de preacher a' tall.

159

We's may even beat him ta where he's going," Ol' Slantface said.

Picking his way through the cacti and stone formations, a discerning man would enter the box canyon to our left and descend a game trail which led to a cirque, or hanging valley. This we did.

The valley was no more than a hundred yards long and fifty wide, but the grass was uncommonly good and the horses could graze and rest for a day. A tank of water was off to the south end of the valley, dripping into a seep full of fresh water, and suddenly everyone knew Ol' Slantface had been here before.

"How is it you know of this place?" Lieutenant Trumann asked out of curiosity.

"I come through here width Carson in fifty-three. I trapped wid him all dat summer. I know where it is we ride."

"Well, I'll be hanged. I never figured you for being that old."

"I wasn't; I was just a kid not much older dan Dillon. I signed on wid de Carson's party trying ta git home. We escaped de ship's Cap'm, much like O'Queda. I's just wanted ta go home. Den one day Carson said a man can't ever go home, not once so much life has happened to him."

"You've learned a bit since then."

There was silence for a while as everyone unsaddled and turned the stock out to graze. As for me, I began to wonder if I could ever go home. Ol' Slantface was looking right at me when he made his remark. He might have been speaking to everyone in the party, but his message was clearly directed right at me. "A man can't ever go home, not once so much life has happened to him." I have never forgotten those words, not to this day.

We built a small fire by the seep and settled in for the night. The Indian boy had gathered wood for the fire, and there was no smoke whatsoever as the twigs and brush burned to catch the larger wood on fire. This amazed me, for I had never myself built a fire that didn't send up some kind of smoke. This valley was an island unto itself, a place where several riders could remain hidden for a good many days, if they stayed still and didn't go traipsing about the countryside.

We camped to one side, away from the seep so the horses could drink whatever water they wanted without being disturbed. There was no easy way out of the valley. No horse but a wild one or a horse being guided by a man would venture the steep rocky terrain necessary to get out. With all the grass and water at their disposal, the consensus was the horses would remain right where they were until we rounded them up in the morning. The army detail, our night watchmen and would stop any animal trying to exit the valley anyway.

The army detachment always posted guard, so the rest of us got a little more rest of an evening. We rested all that evening, then moved out at first light. The shadowy trail which led away from the seep was little more than a game trail. The valley unexpectedly disappeared behind us. Suddenly we navigated down a strange switchback, which emptied out onto a lower plateau. We were headed south toward the Gila River, then east toward the bend. Once we made the river, we would have water for the next several days. The preacher could poison all the waterholes he wanted, but he couldn't poison an entire river.

When the Civil War arrived, the few men who knew of the valley and seep were killed in the fighting back east; save for one, Ol' Slantface. So this was how the water had been forgotten by all but the occasional Pima or Apache Indian who had stumbled upon the hidden water valley. The strange thing was, had I been an Indian I would have lived right there. The valley was green and beautiful, full of water and anything else needed to sustain life. Wild game seemed to be all that visited the place though.

As a great throng of peaks danced before us, we picked our way down the narrow slope into another valley, but this one held little brush and no grass. Continually the men in our party looked over their shoulders, at any moment expecting to see Indians watching, but we never saw any sign of another human.

"If'n dey is an Indian watching, you won't see him no way," Slantface informed the group. "Dey's like no udder group of people on earth. Dey can sneak right up ta ya and ya wouldn't know it. Take dat Indian boy fo' instance. He was sitting in camp staring at us before anybody even know'd he was dere. If'n Indians come, dey be little ta no warning."

"What you're saying is, we've been lucky so far," Lieutenant Trumann replied.

"Uncommon lucky; I don't know how we missed dem up ta dis point," my partner said, shaking his head from side to side.

Everyone was quiet as we rode ahead, only now we were jumpy. Anything that moved drew our attention, the wind blowing a scrub, a lizard or snake, a rabbit scared from cover. We were miserable men as we rode toward the Gila River. Then we spied the water up ahead, and suddenly we were happy again, for the watercourse had been much closer than we had expected. As we drew nigh the river we came upon a marked grave withered by the years of neglect.

HERE LIES
JACK DEAL
DIED 1853

"Howdy, Pop, been a long time," Ol' Slantface said. Abruptly, we knew why we had come this way—at least one of the reasons. Everyone gave the former slave trader his space as we watered our stock. Finally, at daybreak we started east, heading upstream along the riverbank. The night before Ol' Slantface had tidied up around his father's grave. Suddenly, I found myself identifying with the man in more and more ways. I had the feeling he had lost family the hard way, and now I knew. Life must have dealt him some tough cards, and we were witness to the fact he had survived to become a tower of strength and intimidation. He was a very smart man.

Giving thought as we pulled out, I realized the preacher was the only man who wasn't bothered by Ol' Slantface. Why was the preacher different? Was it because he was really the evil one, or was he too stupid to be afraid of the man? I studied on the preacher then, because I couldn't see how anybody couldn't be afraid of Ol' Slantface, but I wasn't.

The trail led upward along a ridge overlooking the river. Ol' Slantface started his horse up, and the lieutenant followed. The three of us boys fell in behind, and the rest of the army brought up the rear. We climbed the ridge, then started back down, riding along a cliff overlooking the river. The edge broke away sharply, and we found ourselves fairly halted by the spectacular view over the Gila. We were about three hundred feet above the river, and we could see for miles in both directions.

"Dis is where we camp fo' de night. Lieutenant, see dat you ration de remaining food. De next several days, game will be scarce unless we catch some fish from de river," Ol' Slantface raised his voice to ensure everyone heard.

"Secure your horses, men, or they'll likely take off in the night, looking for the valley we stayed in last night. We can't afford to be afoot come morning," Lieutenant Trumann instructed.

We secured the horses to the back wall of the shelf, and made ready our camp. The soldiers didn't leave the securing of our horses to us boys; they took over and secured them for us, not wanting to have to chase down even one of the animals come morning.

There was no wood where we were, so we had a dry camp that evening. The men didn't want to risk a fire anyway. If we lit one, it was likely Indians would see it from afar and become curious. We didn't want to alert even one set of stray eyes to our presence.

That evening I struggled, tossed and turned in my sleep, running from the nightmare's which suddenly infested my mind. The devil was nearer than I figured and in my dreams, he was the preacher. He was haunting me in my sleep, and he was after me. I ran every time he came into view, but I couldn't shake him. No matter where I hid from my nemesis, he showed up to do me in. He began to grow horns from his forehead near his temple, one on each side. They weren't big like the horns on a cow, but they became a more prominent feature each time he exposed one of my hiding places. I couldn't seem to get away from the evil that was the preacher Jeremiah Culpepper. At times he was surrounded by demons or minions; their only purpose seemed to be pointing me out to the devil himself, always at the very moment he was about to overlook me. I couldn't hide anywhere without being fingered by one of those lousy demons.

Two hours before sunup we were moving again. I was never so glad to be awakened early in all my life. My destruction had been imminent, and awakening from my sleep had been all that saved me, so I believed at the time. Somehow in my dream, the preacher had grown into a monster with ten heads and horns on every one of them. He breathed fire, and his destruction was swift and final. I can't explain how I managed to escape over and over again, but I did realize; anything is possible in your dreams!

By late in the afternoon on the third day, we had reached the Gila River Bend. From there, we turned due north following the river and headed toward the community of Prescott. If we didn't cross the preacher's tracks once we left the Gila River Valley, according to Slantface, we would know he had turned north. If we did cross his trail, we would fall in behind once again.

Five days later, we found the town of Palo Verde. The preacher had been there. When he left out several days earlier, he had headed due north. So once again we were on his trail. From Palo Verde we followed a no name creek to Skull Valley, just shy of Prescott. The preacher was still a few days ahead of us, but we had not lost much ground. He was heading north again, which was true to my partner's way of thinking. At Prescott we missed him by only a day, so we freshened up, sent a message to San Francisco by overland stage, and headed north as soon as we could.

Our Indian never went into town with us. He was afraid what the white men would think, so he stayed shy of towns. At Prescott, O'Queda stayed with him, and I was the only boy who accompanied the party into town. As such, I was privy to things the other boys missed. Things like the two old men down by the general store talking about going after the preacher, thinking he was hiding a good deal of money.

"Slim, I think we should go. We'll never see that much money in these parts again."

"I'm not so sure. That man is mean, I can feel it."

"He shot me," I interrupted, startling the two men.

"Where did you come from, boy?"

"Does it matter? I heard what you're planning. You'd better hire an army," I said and walked away. I had no idea whether they would listen to a little boy or not, but I gave it a try. Who knows, maybe I saved their lives.

When we rode out of town an hour later, those same two men were watching us with acute attention. I had attempted to discourage them. Whether or not my suggestion might work was yet to be seen, but I had my suspicions.

A week later, we had made it to the Grand Canyon. Now, I had seen some canyons in the last few weeks, but never in my wildest imagination did I ever expect to see such a place as this. Anyone who doesn't believe in God has never seen the Grand Canyon. A man could see for what seemed hundreds of miles in all directions. The canyons were deep and wide, the sun showing through the clouds, which weren't much higher than us that day. We sat our horses on the edge, looking at the tracks upon the ground. I knew we had to follow them, but we would be sitting ducks on the side of a cliff if the preacher was down there waiting for us.

"Well, Lieutenant, dis where we earn our keep." Without hesitation Ol' Slantface turned his mount and headed down the narrow canyon trail. We fell in behind, noting it was a long way to the bottom if somebody slipped. At points we had to dismount and lead our horses behind us. At others, we had to cover the eyes of our horses, because they were scared and wouldn't move an inch until we did so. At such times as we covered their eyes, we had to lead them for a good ways before they showed any inclination to settle down. They seemed to trust our eyes once we had them blinded. In this way, our horses grew more accustomed to our ways and more trusting of us.

The way things were shaping up, we were still going to be on the side of the canyon wall, a cliff of immense proportions, when the sun went down. There was no way we could do such a thing. We needed the sun and we needed to get off of this cliff. Ol' Slantface seemed to read my thoughts and picked up his pace. We were near the bottom when darkness came, and we continued down until we were on the bottom floor of the great canyon.

There was water here and we made camp, broke out some deer meat we had shot north of Prescott, and settled in for the night. Again my nightmares came after me, the preacher never ceasing in his efforts to finish me off. I tossed and turned by the flicker of campfire light. Again, I was saved by the waking of the men in our camp.

After a week of travel in and around the Grand Canyon, we found ourselves in a place called Wolf Hole in the northwest corner of Arizona territory. Wolf Hole was the sum total of three buildings. The saloon and hotel was all one building and the other was a mercantile; the stable was the third. Each had living quarters upstairs, and there was not even one house to augment the business end of town. There was only one side of anything called a street, while the buildings were fronted by the rising mountains to our west. Someone had marked off a survey across from the hotel, for another building no doubt, but as of yet nothing else had been done. There was no purpose I could see that explained why the town was located in such an out of the way place, unless it was built so the men who lived here could rob unsuspecting travelers. I personally could envision no other excuse for the town's existence.

The direction we had maintained since leaving the Gila River country would have us arriving at the Great Salt Lake within a few weeks. That meant we were near Ute Indian country, and still we had not seen any Indians.

Chapter 13

The horse when we saw it was tied to the hitch rail and was flanked by two stout Missouri mules. They still held their packs, and the horse remained saddled. We had found the preacher! There was no doubt where he was; in the saloon wetting his whistle after a long hard ride.

We sat our horses about fifty yards from Wolf Hole to gather our thoughts and came up with a plan, for we had come upon our adversary unexpectedly. We had suspected we would catch up with him somewhere out on the desert plains or in the mountains. No one had expected to stumble upon him in this manner, and we had no plan that included witnesses or innocent bystanders.

"Dere it is, Lieutenant, all of it. Now how's do we get it?" Ol' Slantface wanted to know.

"I say we just ride up to the hitch rail, untie the mules and ride off."

"We'll git a bullet in our backs 'fore we can go a hundred yards."

"You stay here and cover us. If anyone comes out the front door, you blast them," Trumann instructed.

"All right, we's meet you 'bout three miles north of town," Slantface confirmed.

"Dodge and Keyes, you come with me; the rest of you stay here and cover us," Lieutenant Trumann ordered.

They started up the street, the lieutenant giving instructions as they rode. My hair was on end because I knew there was going to be gunfire. The last time I was around any kind of gunplay, I had been shot or kidnapped, neither an outcome I had liked. The same players were present this time, but I was holding my own weapon now. There simply couldn't be another way. When the preacher saw his mother lode being heisted by the folks he had stolen it from, he was going to come unhinged. He was a trusting sort, to leave those animals standing there like that, but he hadn't seen hide-nor-hair of us for three weeks or better.

I steadied my horse beneath me and held my rifle in the direction of the front door. "Take it easy boys, we don't want ta shoot our own. Dillon, aim high. Aim at de door facing," Slantface ordered. I watched as Dodge and Keyes untied the two mules and slipped their ropes around the saddle horns; then stepping into their stirrups, they were off. With his pistol out and pointed at the front door, Lieutenant Trumann put two bullets into the opening of the saloon and left the street as if his pants were on fire. A moment later, the preacher came running out onto the front porch, gun in hand. As he turned his back to us and levered his gun to take aim, we let him have it. He dove back inside so fast we couldn't tell if we'd hit him or not. Slowly and steadily, the soldiers with us fanned out and continued to put bullets into the front doorway of the saloon, lest the preacher try and leave or get a bullet into the backs of our friends. Slantface had moved around so he could watch the backs of the buildings to make sure no one escaped.

Once the thieves were out of harm's way, Ol' Slantface said, "Let git out of here!" We put spurs to our horses and did as he instructed.

The former slave trader pumped two quick rounds of his own into the backdoor facing of the saloon, and we swung wide around Wolf Hole toward the mountains so we could meet up with the soldiers who had stolen back my father's gold shipment. We maintained a distance of about a half mile as we circled the town, for no one had yet developed a long range weapon which could shoot accurately for such a distance. We watched as the preacher stepped into his saddle and took off after the three soldiers who had lightened his burden. He didn't even look our way.

"Let's go," Slantface yelled, kicking his horse with spurs.

We took off at a dead run, and the only question for me was; who got to kill the preacher? I wanted to, Slantface wanted his chance, and then there was the Indian who said almost nothing, but managed to get his point across most times just by looking at you. The preacher had three mad-as-all-git-out victims closing the gap on him faster than he was able to close the gap on the soldiers who had stolen the gold-laden mules. I had never seen a Missouri mule run all out before, but from what I could tell, they were having no trouble keeping up with the soldier boys on their horses.

We crashed through knee high brush and cacti, leaving plenty of dust in our wake as we closed in on the man who had killed Pa. Then he glanced over his shoulder and made a ninety degree sweeping right angle turn, heading east. Having seen his back trail plastered with angry victims, the money suddenly wasn't so all fired important it seemed.

Slantface lifted his rifle and put two rounds into the ground near the preacher, but we still had too much distance between us to be accurate. For general purposes, I lifted my rifle and added one more as my horse ran like greased lightning. Private Loren added his two cents, and we stayed after the varmint. He was running for his life now, so I was pretty certain he knew who was after him; if not me, he could not mistake Ol' Slantface, his former partner.

Up to now I had completely forgotten the name of the Indian boy, but suddenly I remembered he was called Poke Joy. When we lit out after the preacher, the Indian on his paint horse began to stretch out his legs and pass us all, gaining on the preacher, which I could not explain in any reasonable fashion. He didn't even have a saddle! In no time, he had fifty yards on the bunch of us, and his horse was running like the wind. I knew then who had the fastest horse in our bunch. The preacher looked over his shoulder and saw this developing, so he ducked behind a rock formation and hastily dismounted. When the Indian got close enough, he fired a shot and dropped the boy's horse from under him; then for good measure, the evil in him began to try and shoot Poke Joy, who dove behind his fallen horse and waited.

We pulled up short then. It's one thing to go after an armed man on a horse running at full speed, and quite another to rush a man who's on the ground and can drop you with a very accurate rifle shot. We tied our mounts off, and Slantface began to give orders to circle the preacher's position and move in on him. This was easier said than done, for every time one of us moved, a bullet would kick up dirt in our faces.

There was still about three hundred yards separating us, but Poke Joy was closer at about two. However, he had no rifle, and at this distance nothing else was going to work. Then we saw the Indian begin to move. Slowly and purposefully he maneuvered closer, and for the life of me I couldn't see how he could do such a thing without getting shot. At times he would stop for ten or twenty minutes and lie perfectly still, but then he would begin to edge closer. How was he doing this? Couldn't the preacher see him coming?

I remembered what Ol' Slantface had said, "By the time you see them coming, it'll be too late."

How could the Poke Joy be so sneaky? I could see him easily, as could all of us; why couldn't the preacher? I watched intently as Poke Joy lay still for almost an hour, and then moved again. Suddenly I got it! He was not moving as long as the preacher was facing his direction; he blended in with the terrain because of his sun darkened skin, and if he wasn't moving he couldn't be seen. When the preacher looked away, that was when he moved forward, inching ever closer to his prey; but if he got to him, what then? He was just a boy and I knew what the preacher was capable of.

Suddenly, for no reason I could decipher, the preacher mounted up and rode off to the north. I wasn't sure if he didn't like the odds, if he spotted the young Indian boy, or if he had developed a plan to get the gold back from the soldiers, but Culpepper was gone.

Poke Joy stood and watched inquisitively as the preacher rode away. The rest of us mounted up and went to pick the Indian up. Poke Joy mounted behind me, and we trailed the preacher north. As long as he was out there, we were sitting ducks. When I picked Poke Joy up, he had only been fifty yards shy of the rock formation the preacher had been hiding behind. This impressed me. The Indian boy was a good stalker.

The trail led to a spot where the Santa Clara River joined the Virgin River just northeast of the Virgin Mountains. Instead of three miles from Wolf Hole, the soldiers had traveled near twenty before we caught up with them. I learned something about Ol' Slantface then. I had seen other men on the trail, but none of them could match him. Time and again, when I would lose the trail, he would pick up sign, seeming to know more by instinct than by anything he saw on the ground which way they had gone. They had a campfire burning and were setting down to supper, waiting on us.

"Did you boys git lost?" Ol' Slantface asked.

"Not exactly," Lieutenant Trumann responded. "We hadn't figured on all that shooting. When we looked back, the preacher was coming our way, so we figured we'd better put some dust into the air. We needed a good spot to defend. One where he couldn't sneak up on us—this was it."

Looking around, Slantface gave his approval. "Plenty of water, wide open country; nope, I's don't reckon he'll be able ta sneak up on us."

"Now what do we do?" The lieutenant asked.

"We's in Utah Territory, dat means hell. We gone from anywhere civilization might be easy ta get to." Taking out his parchment map, Ol' Slantface began to look and I was looking over his shoulder. "We two thousand miles from New Orleans, maybe fifteen hundred from Kansas City and seventeen hundred from St. Louie as de crow flies."

"So, we're looking at two months or better of travel, whether we take a boat around the horn or ride straight through Indian Territory all the way to Louisiana," Lieutenant Trumann observed.

"You's correct, Lieutenant; de question is, which way do we's go?"

"Back to San Diego, catch a ship and notify the rest of the men in San Francisco that we have recovered the gold. Our mission now is to get the gold into the proper hands as soon as possible."

"All right, we ride back ta Wolf Hole in de morning," my partner agreed.

Nobody talked less than Ol' Slantface then, except maybe the Indian, who never spoke anyway. You can learn a lot about a man by riding the trail with him. For the last few months, I had gotten to know Ol' Slantface pretty good, and he wasn't really a bad man at all. At least he had a heart, which was more than I could say for the preacher, Jeremiah Culpepper. Ol' Slantface never wasted a motion, never took unnecessary chances, and scouted every potential ambush before riding in. He never made light of what he was doing, and never made a point other than letting his actions speak for him.

When Pa died, the cabin on Current River reverted to me, but if he left any money behind I didn't know about it. Pa had worked his entire life, only to be killed by the likes of Jeremiah Culpepper. I had my father's Confederate pistol and gun-belt, which was now mine, and the rifle he had used to hold off the preacher. I had picked it up at the ambush site back on the Natchez Trace; but other than that, I had nothing to remind me of my heritage. There had been a medallion in Pa's pocket. Somehow those thieves had overlooked it, so I held onto it for a keepsake, but there simply hadn't been anything else to keep.

The following day, we rode back into Wolf Hole with two Missouri mules and a gold shipment meant for the Confederate States of America. It seemed to me Wolf Hole's sole purpose for being was to relieve unsuspecting travelers of their wares and goods, to rob good decent folk of their personal property. Slantface figured to give them their chance. I knew, as well as did everyone, where we were. The Indian wanted to be dropped off outside of town as usual, so I let him down and we went on in. That Indian was the joker in the deck. He was going to get his shot at the preacher come hell or high water, and it appeared he was going to get the initial chance. Suddenly the preacher had turned up missing, but I knew he would reveal himself to us again. I didn't figure to give him that chance.

In this matter, I was becoming jealous, because I wanted first shot at killing the vermin who had killed my father, and all indicators pointed to the fact that it would in all likelihood be Poke Joy who got a chance to finish him off first. We stabled our horses in the barn and brought the gold in through the crowded saloon to our room upstairs. There was quite an ostentatious display of weaponry as we made our way up the stairs. The gold was placed in the room under guard. As we were climbing the stairs, I suddenly realized that recovering the gold had been one thing; keeping it was going to be quite something else altogether.

The men in the saloon were licking their lips, just beating their brains trying to figure a way they could relieve us of all that gold. No one had to explain to me what they were thinking. I could tell by the look on their faces, they wanted what we had. They already knew what was in those bags; we weren't fooling anyone. To get possession, they would have to murder six men and three boys. Some of the characters I spied in the room looked capable of doing just that and then some, especially the one who sat in the back corner wearing a patch over one eye, while his other eyed us with malice.

This was the wildest example of a man I had ever laid eyes on. Unshaven and dirty, he shuffled a worn deck of old cards. His countenance was one of pure meanness. There was nothing about him that gave anyone a hint of civilization. His clothes were bear skins, likely because no one made anything big enough that would stretch around him. He gave me the willies.

We ate in shifts, but the downstairs room was quiet; we didn't talk and neither did the men who shared the saloon with us. The room was filled with smoke from cigars and cigarettes and the smell of chewing tobacco, but we ate our fill. There was a picture of a half-naked woman on one wall and a cattle puncher roping a cow on another. The bar was backed with a long mirror and bright shiny glasses, way too many for such a nowhere place as Wolf Hole. I didn't understand this. It was as if the man who owned the bar was taking his wares to San Francisco, and along the way, he changed his mind and just set everything up here. Here was in the middle of nowhere. Everything was too nice for such country as this part of the frontier.

I studied things, along with the other men in the room, as I ate. Nothing I witnessed gave me comfort. If we made San Diego without being assaulted, I would count my lucky stars, but I knew better. We were going to be lucky to get fifty miles without some of the men in this room trying to shoot us down and take what we were transporting. For the first time, I began to realize what Pa had been up against. The task seemed impossible to me, but then I did have Ol' Slantface, who thought better than most men, and right then I began to hope he was as good as I believed he was.

The preacher was nowhere to be found, and if he did show up, there was an Indian waiting for him before he ever got into town. So I eased my conscience about the preacher for a spell and studied the men in the room. I had the impression some of them rode together, although they were not sitting together. They didn't have uniforms like the soldiers who rode with us, but the way they were dressed and the length of time they had been wearing the same clothes; this was responsible for the way I sized them up more than anything. And then there was the big man sitting back in the corner playing solitaire with a well-used deck of cards; so well-used they must be the deck he carried with him wherever he went. The card player with the eye patch was the meanest-looking man in the room next to Ol' Slantface, and several times I had witnessed my partner stare him down, though the man would stack up as two of anybody.

Finally we exited the room by the way of the stairs and gave the other men a chance to eat. There were three rooms between us because Ol' Slantface didn't want to make things easy for anyone who might try to break in and shoot it out. Not knowing which room the gold was in would slow any would-be thieves down a good deal. Three men to a room and two in the last meant someone would be up at all times, and the hope was that we could keep them guessing. No one in their right mind would begin an attack unless they knew where the gold was. Logic and reason would say it had to be in the middle one, but that went right out the window the longer you thought about it. There just wasn't any way for anyone to know, short of beating the answer out of one of our party.

We got through the night without incident and had a hearty breakfast, because our trip was going to be weeks of traveling with scarce food and water. Every one of us knew the route we would take, because the route was the same one we had taken to get here, only in reverse. We saddled up and secured the gold to the mules, then rode out of Wolf Hole the way we came, and we were primed for trouble. There wasn't a horse in town but for ours; something we had noticed while saddling up. Every man in town had left ahead of us, including the hotel manager and bartender, leaving only the female cook. And we also had to consider the preacher. He would be out there somewhere, waiting on us.

As we headed south, we expected to see Poke Joy walking out to meet us, but for awhile he never did. We kept the horses pointed in the direction we had come, and sure enough, pretty soon here came our Indian down from the hills, getting his hide down to where we were riding. He walked up to Ol' Slantface. "Five white men over next hill," he said, pointing the way we were going.

"Can you lead us around them?" Ol' Slantface asked.

"Can you ride horse?"

"You know I can ride, what's dat ta do wid..?" Ol' Slantface trailed off, realizing the Indian boy was laughing at him. "Get aback of me; you ride point today."

Poke Joy jumped up behind Ol' Slantface who led off to the southeast around another hill. We rode far around

Diamond Butte and came to Cold Springs Wash. Following the wash, which was dry this time of year, we split the mountains Trumbull and Logan then passed by Mt. Emma and Mt. Dellenbaugh. Once again, we had entered the Grand Canyon. We had to navigate the cliffs to get down into the valley, so we decided to wait until morning.

The following evening, we camped on the south side of the Colorado River. We had covered a good forty miles on horseback, and if nothing else, we had the desperados guessing where we had gotten to. If they figured out what we'd done, they'd still have to cross the river to reach us. They couldn't do that quietly, not in the dark, they couldn't. Five men accounted for pretty much everybody in the town of Wolf Hole, including the Mayor, if they even had one. I wondered if the hotel manager wasn't the lead man. Then I remembered the big wide man with the eye patch in the corner and changed my mind. He would be the ramrod of any bunch coming after us.

We set up the guard that evening, and for the first time us civilians stood watch along with the soldiers, a double watch so there could be no mistakes. Ol' Slantface took the first and last watch leaving myself, O'Queda and Poke Joy to stand the three watches in between. One man was to stay with the horses at all times, while the other watched the gold. We couldn't finish the trip without horses, and we wouldn't finish it without the gold.

In the morning, we sat up to a hot cup of coffee and warmed our bones around the driftwood fire, using wood Poke Joy had gathered. Everyone was looking around at one another when Ol' Slantface came walking in from the horses. He grabbed his cup from his saddlebag and filled it with boiling coffee and then leaned back against his saddle.

"Poke Joy, you picked up English fast enough," he accused.

"White girl in our village; she has taught me much."

"No wonder. I shoulda asked dat first night in camp, but I'd udder things on my mind."

Well, such a thing was possible, for it was not unusual for a white girl to be raised by Indians if her family had been killed in an Indian raid. There had been several stories which had gotten back to the civilized folks back east, where a young girl was kidnapped and raised as a squaw. Sometimes they got away and came back on their own. I remember hearing one story about a mountain man who had come upon just such a situation while trading with the Comanche and ended up trading for a young white girl who had been held captive for nearly three years. She had lost her family in the raid when the Indians took her hostage, so she had no family to go home to. The mountain man, by the name of "Old Bill" Williams, married her then settled down in St. Louis never trapping fur again. Last I heard, they had nine children and counting.

Fur trappers still used St. Louis for their home. The Civil War had slowed things down a bit, but once the war ended, operations with the fur trading companies, such as the Hudson Bay Company, would resume full scale. I found it hard to believe, but the standing legend was fur trappers who sold their wares in St. Louis the last ten years had collected over four million dollars for their efforts. We were carrying two hundred and fifty thousand in gold, so I couldn't even imagine four million.

There was no shortage of places in St. Louis to spend such money either; I had seen that much during my three-day stay a few months back. The waterfront was lined with taverns, grogshops and houses of ill repute. The local Soulard Farmers Market was there also, and you never saw a farmer's market so big. On Saturday, you could buy just about anything that was in season and some things that were not. I remembered walking through the market with my sister, and all we had was two bits between us, but there was a colorfully dressed young lady who felt sorry for us and gave us something to eat, telling me to keep my money, for I might need it later.

St. Louis was where everyone congregated. The fur trappers, soldiers who had returned from the war crippled and maimed, soldiers shipping off to war to fight for the Federals, and river men who operated the boats on the Mississippi and Missouri Rivers. There were gamblers of every kind, wagoneer's who assembled mighty wagon trains to head west, the folks who were headed west, and then there were the orphans; twenty thousand of them since the start of the war with more arriving every day. It hadn't taken me long to figure out that the section known as "the Cauldron" was the life of the town and a possible terror at the same time. The streets of St. Louis during the Civil War were not fit for anyone's safety, let alone the orphaned children. There had been three murders of young ladies in the few days I was there, and those crimes went unsolved.

The city had no less than three newspapers, at least one book store and an art gallery. There was a show every night in one theater or another; fifty plays this year alone, and the year was not over. There were parties for rich folks, weddings, dances and the like to keep anyone who wanted entertainment entertained. There was a fight every five minutes on the waterfront, and by the time Jenny and I left town I viewed them as a form of entertainment, as did most everyone else.

There had been a duel on Blood Island while I was in town; both men had died at the hand of their opponent. One of them had been the richest man in town, although I never got his name. Each had left behind a widow and a fortune. The widow of a great man known as Daniel Webster lived on the outskirts of town somewhere, but he was not one of the men involved in the duel. These were the things I remembered as I sat beside the fire that evening wondering what was to happen next.

Chapter 14

Our party of gold snatchers left the Colorado River an hour before sunup. Once again Poke Joy was riding behind me, for the mules were too laden with gold to risk adding weight to their burden. Private Dodge had the point, followed by Ol' Slantface, Private Loren, Corporal Keyes and then me. O'Queda rode behind us, then Sergeant Ward, and finally Lieutenant Trumann. Slantface had one of the mules roped around his saddle horn, and Trumann had the other.

We rode slow and cautious, carefully scouting any place which seemed fitting for an ambush. Likely those men back yonder were still coming behind us, but we couldn't be sure. They might have circled around us in the night and found a place where they could lie in wait for an unsuspecting crew, but we weren't unsuspecting. For this reason we rode with purpose.

A week later, by way of the Juniper Mountains, we rode into Prescott and sent a letter to San Francisco telling Captain James Endicott we had recovered the gold and to meet us in San Diego. We had no way of knowing if he would get the message on time, but we had to try. There was the wire to San Francisco, but it was well to the north of us.

In 1860, the Pony Express, formed by Russell, Majors and Waddell, set records for mail between St. Joe and San Francisco, but the rub I learned from Slantface was this: When the first rider rode out of St. Joe, there were reporters on hand from London, Paris and New York. Their job was to tell the story to the folks back home. Now, they told the story, but the amazing thing was, they described how the mail arrived on the Highball train. They described the train ride, how the train was refueled with wood in less than five minutes, how it sped in excess of sixty miles an hour to make up for lost time in order to deliver the express package to the first rider on time. They did all of that but they couldn't describe the rider who had ridden out of St. Joe that day. Slantface said it was because the rider was a little colored boy, and no black boy could be the new face of an American hero. The Pony Express had advertised for orphans to put their line together, and they didn't care if the orphan was black or white; they just didn't want to have to write a letter home to someone's family if one of the riders got killed riding through Indian Territory.

I was learning a lot from Ol' Slantface, and right then I figured I could do a lot worse than to hang around him for a while. I doubted whether my own father could have taught me the things I had learned in just a few months riding with the former slave trader from New Orleans.

Now, the telegraph had put the Pony Express out of business. The Pony Express was for all intents and purposes bankrupt. The mail line had been a good idea at the time, but in less than two years, the Messenger Company was in trouble, and all it had taken was a single little wire stretched across the plains and mountains from Kansas City to San Francisco.

The railroads didn't run that far yet, but all indications were that they would eventually run from coast to coast once the war was over and the country could get back to work. For now, the train line was only as far west as Stillwater, Oklahoma.

The way Ol' Slantface was imparting his knowledge to us boys, for I wasn't the only one learning, never seemed like he was preaching, just talking to the wind, not to anyone in particular. I bet the men who rode with us were learning a thing or two themselves. Even if he had been preaching at us, I'd have listened. Ol' Slantface was the type of storyteller who made you sit up and hang on every word he had to say. When I measured the preacher man alongside my partner, the preacher sure seemed to come out on the short end of the stick in every way that counted, but he won hands down when it came to pure meanness.

In Prescott, we again settled into three rooms, this time at the Crescent hotel, and Ol' Slantface bought a fresh horse for Poke Joy. I had to wonder how common was the name Crescent? It had been the name of our ship as well. The young Indian had shown to be such a good tracker, Ol' Slantface outfitted him with a new saddle, a rifle and saddlebags. The horse was a line back dun and looked like he could outrun the wind. As it turned out he could. I was still jealous of Poke Joy because once again he had the best horse among us.

I had no right to be jealous, but there seemed to be a tinge of jealousy in my heart when Poke Joy stepped into his saddle the following morning outside of town. He pranced around in a circle a few times and spun around to look at us, just to show off.

"White man knows how to pick horse," he said.

"Correction; black man," Ol' Slantface argued.

Poke Joy looked at him like he didn't understand, and he didn't. To him, all men who were not Indians were considered white. He would learn different, but for now it didn't matter. He was a very happy boy. Riding in leather grew on him rapidly.

We didn't stay in Prescott any longer than was necessary to get a good night's rest, so by about ten in the morning we were a good fifteen miles south, riding in the wide open spaces of hills and desert. There were tall pines here and there, but we stayed out in the open, where we could see for miles, and tried to keep a good distance away from the trees, in case any bandits were hiding in them. When the trees began to close in on us, we sent a soldier to the left and to the right to ride ahead and signal if they saw anything. We stayed in the middle of the wide open country and kept riding south.

Late in the evening, we found an arroyo and made camp out of sight from any would-be travelers, friendly or otherwise. The creek bed was well-hidden on all four sides because of two ninety degree turns very close to one another. We were able to draw in all of the horses and build a good fire in the thirty-foot-deep ravine. Private Dodge had shot a running wolf earlier in the day, scattering the pack from the area. I had never seen a wolf dressed in any way, shape or form; I didn't even know they were edible; but apparently they were downright good eating, because we didn't leave any leftovers.

Private Dodge had some kind of concoction which he called a marinade; different spices all mixed in a vinegar and oil solution, which he said "draws out the flavor." To me, if you draw something out, it meant whatever you were drawing out wouldn't be there when your steaks were done, but I was wrong. He meant the exact opposite. He said the purpose for his concoction was to draw out the flavor or bring it to the surface, so a man could taste the meat. If ever I understood the English language, I didn't understand this, not at first, anyway.

We stayed fairly warm in our well-hidden camp, letting the fire burn well into the night. The horses were secure, and everyone got what we figured was good sleep. Come morning, we fixed coffee and wet our whistle before kicking out the fire, secured the packs to the mules, checked our weapons and saddled up. Not one of us believed we would get through another day without some type of altercation, but we guessed wrong.

A few more days saw us to the Gila River, where we had been a few weeks earlier. What I couldn't figure was why no one had bothered us yet. Then it dawned on me that the farther from any civilization we rode, the better any would-be crooks would like it. Those men from Wolf Hole would be coming right along. We'd managed to dodge them once, but now they would be riding to overtake us at a spot which made sense for them. I was comforted by the fact that there wasn't anywhere to ambush us until we left the river a few days farther down the stream.

Poke Joy was riding off to see if he could find game for us to eat, scouting from the high mountain peaks and so on; any excuse that offered him a chance to use his new horse found him in the saddle and gone. I understood this, because he had never owned such a fine animal, and no Indian in his tribe had probably ever laid eyes on one so good as the creature Ol' Slantface had bought for him. If Poke Joy wasn't careful, he was going to ride the hair right off of him.

I never dreamed that the quickest way back to New Orleans would be to ride in an opposite direction for several weeks then catch a boat, but this made sense if a man thought about things just a little bit. We would have been months on the trail if we'd headed east directly.

We spent a week on the river, taking our time not pushing our horses at all, trying to let those men behind us catch up. They never did. If they were following us, there was nary a sign of them. Poke Joy had ridden back several times to check our back trail, and there was no one coming. He would ride into camp of an evening and tell us what he'd seen, but never did he witness the fact we might be followed; not along the river.

I thought a lot about Jenny that week, wondering how she was getting along with Mrs. Danbury. I was thankful the preacher was out here somewhere and not back in Missouri, where he could be trouble for my little sister. I also wondered about the preacher. How could a man with so much evil in him get up in front of a congregation on Sunday morning, all smiles and laughter, and give a sermon from the Bible? All of my life I had been taught evil could come to no good end, yet the preacher seemed not to be angering God in the least. He was getting away with murder, theft and God knows what else. This didn't seem right to me at all. It was then I made a pact with myself to keep an eye on how things turned out for the preacher.

We moved into the hanging valley just north of the Gila River by the end of the week, and still we hadn't seen hide nor hair of Jeremiah Culpepper, nor the men from Wolf Hole. What worried me most was if they found each other and joined forces. I wanted the preacher to myself, not surrounded by a bunch of money-hungry thieves.

As before, we let our horses have the run of the valley, for there was plenty of good grass and no good way out, but by late evening we had staked them near our camp. Poke Joy rode in late and said, "White man come."

Well, he didn't have to explain what white man; we all knew there was only one who would be anywhere near our current position. He was not coming down the Gila, but coming around the mountains to head us off. By morning, he would surely have accomplished this, and while we were sitting around figuring what we should or shouldn't do, Poke Joy mounted up and rode to head him off at the pass; literally.

I got up from the campfire and saddled my horse, then walked him over to the spring and let him drink. Ol' Slantface looked at me and said, "Where you going?"

"If the Indian misses, I won't," I said, and stepped into the saddle.

"Be careful, Dillon, I still need you," he said.

Well, I looked at him then and wondered just what he was talking about. He needed me? Of all the things to say, that one made the least amount of sense. Ol' Slantface was a man what didn't need anyone at all, not to my way of thinking. What could he possibly need me for, slowing him down? Well, sir, I just looked at him.

Finally, I spun my horse around and headed up the valley. I was wasting time, and I sure enough had me a preacher to kill. If Poke Joy managed to do the job first, I still planned to put a couple of bullets into his carcass, just out of pure meanness. Now, for the first time in my life, I was deliberately stalking a man. Well, he might be a man, but to me he was evil incarnate, the devil himself.

I worked my way up to the north end of the valley, and started to climb. The trail out wasn't easy to see in the dark, but I managed. Three times my horse slipped going up, and I began to wonder just what I was doing. You can't sneak up on a man making the kind of noise I was making. It was then I remembered to give the horse his head, I was trying too hard; and he didn't have any more missteps after that.

"I still need you!" Now why did Ol' Slantface have to go and say something to throw me all out of whack? He could have said anything but that.

As I crested the hill, my horse slipped one last time, caught his footing and pulled us the rest of the way up. Looking at the trail gave me no comfort. Stepping down, I led my horse; the last thing I wanted was any more slipping. If he slipped on the way down, we'd both meet at the bottom, and I would likely be dead. We kept to the trail for what seemed like a long time, and suddenly I saw the Indian. He was out on the flat moving right along.

The trail took its last bend near the bottom, and I realized how tired I was from the day's travel. When I reached the bottom, I almost stopped and waited on the sun, but I crawled back into the saddle instead. Poke Joy had done the same as me, walking his horse to the bottom, and I took off after him. Out here on the sandy flats, my horse wasn't going to slip and fall, and Poke Joy's trail was fresh in the light of an almost full moon. In the distance I could still see the Indian heading due north, but I knew he would soon disappear into the night. I kept my head, let my horse have his, and we began to track Poke Joy straight toward Castle Dome Peak.

After a few more hours in the saddle, I was good and tired. Poke Joy and his new horse were setting the pace, a pace I was having trouble keeping up with. Then I saw where Poke Joy's tracks fell into lock step with another horse then trailed right up to the dome. Had Jeremiah Culpepper's tracks followed Poke Joy's, I figured it would mean the preacher came after, but the Indian had adjusted his direction to follow the tracks on the ground. It was only my intuition which told me he was following the preacher, though I had no hard evidence to back up my deduction.

At the base of Castle Dome I drew up. Looking down, I could see the others had stopped here too. How far ahead were they? I stared up at the dome, for it was shadowed and still; I could discern no movement. Suddenly I realized that if the two were up on the side of the dome somewhere, I would easily be spotted. Nudging my horse, we began to climb. Once in the rocks, tracking in the dark was impossible. Finding a likely spot near the bottom, I stepped down and waited, listening for any movement up ahead. All I could hear was my horse breathing.

Instantaneously, in the early morning hours of pre-dawn, the night was ripped apart by gunfire. My horse and I both jumped, for the sound had been close; then a bullet trimmed my shoulder, and I grabbed up my saddle horn and mounted. Obviously a ricochet bullet had parted my shirt, and I was now bleeding. I pushed my toes further into the stirrup and hung on, letting my horse have his head.

Leaning low in my saddle for fear of another ricochet, I took control and began to guide my mount up the side of the hill, not knowing where we were headed. If my horse was like me, he wanted away from the gunfire, which had now settled down. After a minute, I heard another lone shot slug the night air, then after a few quiet moments, another. Suddenly, just as the gunfire had started, there was nothing. Up the hill we went, taking a sudden turn into the rocks on our right where I stepped down. My horse had led me to cover behind a big boulder, and I staked him beside me. I would have to wait until morning when I could actually see something. In the dark, I was just a sitting duck with clipped wings.

As the sun began to rise, I could tell I had only been grazed and the bleeding was slight, but in the dark my imagination had me on the verge of dying once again. My horse had landed me on a cliff-side, looking down. There was a body down there. I could see more clearly now, and it was Poke Joy. Instantly my spirit seemed lightened, as if it were going to leave my body, but as I stared at him, I also began to settle down. The preacher was still on the dome!

I looked around my position, yet I could see no sign of Poke Joy's horse and saddle. Likely, the preacher knew a good horse when he saw one and had commandeered the poor beast. With two horses, he could run down anyone he wanted. Heck, he didn't even need his horse anymore; Poke Joy's line-back dun could out run the wind.

Noticing movement off to my left I saw a man working his way down to my friend, and it was not the preacher. It was the man who had been sitting back in the corner at Wolf Hole. "We got him," he yelled back up the hill. I risked a look in the direction of his yell and saw four more men, along with the preacher. Did they know I was here? They hadn't been shooting at me, but they had wounded me just the same. What about my tracks? I didn't think I had been anywhere close to the spot where Poke Joy now lay. Slowly I eased back into the rocks.

Those men from Wolf Hole had obviously waited, and maybe even baited, Poke Joy to ride in this direction. Now they had killed my friend, and I was next if I didn't watch my step. They were making so much noise on the mountain, I didn't figure they would hear my horse if he nickered or stomped his feet, so I settled in to wait. It was clear; they had chosen this spot to ambush our party. If they retreated back to their original position on the mountain at all during the day, I was going to be smoked out. They would see a third set of tracks, and I would be hunted like a dog.

I fell asleep. I was so dog-tired from traveling all day and night. I fell asleep in the shade of the rocks and only awoke when they kicked me. I was so mad at myself for dozing off in those rocks and for being so careless. Those men who had me didn't have to punish me at all; I was doing a fair job of punishing myself sure enough.

"Look what we got here, preacher," one of them was saying.

"Well, boy, you and me, we go way back, way back..." he said. "How about you tell me how far back the rest of your friends are?"

"You mean Slantface and the Army?" I stalled. I should have been scared—wetting my pants scared, but instead I was mad clear through.

"You know exactly who I mean."

I was busy looking at my situation. They had my guns, my horse and they had me, all wrapped up pretty as you please, but I wasn't tied up. The problem was, I couldn't outrun a bullet. Likely I couldn't outrun them either. Every man in the circle around me was from the saloon in Wolf Hole. I now began to catalog them in my mind, because if I was going to live, I had to take care of every single one of them.

"Come on, boy, where are they?"

"What time of day is it?" I asked sheepishly.

"Late afternoon; your snoring is what gave you away," the preacher advised me.

"They're close."

"How close?" the preacher said, and kicked me.

"Real close," I said, but I really had no idea. Buzzards were circling overhead, and I realized they hadn't buried the Indian. "If you didn't bury Poke Joy, you made a mistake. They already know where you are."

"What are you talking about, boy?"

I pointed to the sky above, and the preacher cursed. "You think you're smart, don't you? Well, if you are so smart, why do we have you cornered like the rat you are?"

"I never claimed to be smart, but Ol' Slantface, he's smart. He'll find you."

"His name is Lucifer Deal," the preacher corrected.

"Lucifer," ol' one eye spouted. "Don't you think that's information you should have shared before roping us into this deal?"

"He ain't the devil, he's just a man," the preacher argued.

He kicked me in the thigh and turned away. "Tie him up," he shouted to the other men. "And make sure he's tied tight. I don't want him getting loose and warning the others. The rest of you, get that Indian buried!" When he finished talking he gave me the old evil eye.

I didn't know if my friends were close enough to see the buzzards or not, but my guess was they could be seen for a long way off. If they rode back the way we came, they weren't coming this way anyhow. My only hope at the moment, these men would have to sleep, and I would be wide awake after sleeping all day. It wasn't much, but it might be my only chance to get away—provided I lived that long.

Chapter 15

The stars had come out to wink at me, and as I knew they must, the men had fallen asleep. We hadn't moved from the position I had chosen, because it offered the best cover on Castle Dome. There was no fire burning, and I noticed the men were exhausted. I knew my captors were more tired than I had been. They were snoring to beat the dickens, and I was now wide awake.

They hadn't tied my feet, so as my mind wondered how to get undone, I realized how hungry my horse was. Surely it wasn't possible, but maybe, just maybe, he could help me. I got up and tiptoed over to him turning my back, and lifting my tied wrist to his nose. He sniffed the rope which bound my hands a couple of times, but turned his head away. How hungry was he? I hadn't fed him or let him forage in nearly twenty-four hours. There was a chance. Alas, my idea seemed lost him.

I didn't know if a horse would nibble at my rope bonds or not. This took entirely too long, but eventually he had given a few good tugs upon the rope, trying to get at the hemp bindings which held my hands behind my back. Suddenly, I found the slack I needed and slipped my left hand free. I unraveled my hands and quietly picked up my saddle. Even the man posted as night sentry had fallen asleep. Being not too big a fool, I didn't try to saddle up right there. I made enough noise just getting my saddle up onto my shoulder. I carried it down the hill a ways and went back for my horse and guns.

When I got back into the camp, my own horse had done the unthinkable and already had the knot of rope in his stomach. I had no idea what such a thing might do to him, so I took the horse I knew to be the fastest and eased my way out of camp. The preacher was going to be mad at those fellows, but it served them right. I got to the bottom of the dome, saddled up, shoved my rifle into the scabbard and stepped into the stirrup.

Such a wide open country as this could scare a boy, I knew right then. The only reason I wasn't fearful of dying out here was because of the men I rode with. I knew they would be coming right along behind us. I knew they were close. Carefully I back-tracked my trail until I came to a point where I saw their trail. Where they veered to the west after following our trail as far as made sense, I turned in behind them and started making up for lost time. In three hours I found their camp.

South of the Castle Dome Mountains runs what is called the Castle Dome Plain, and it butts up against the Colorado River. This is where I found my friends. I hailed the camp and rode in just shy of sun-up. I wasn't really tired, but I knew I was about to be. The preacher was coming, and through no fault of my own I was lucky to be breathing. It had been seven kinds of foolishness for me to think I could tackle such a man alone. I thought about it while unsaddling my new horse.

"Look what de cat dragged in," Ol' Slantface said, as I turned to the fire and laid out my blanket roll.

"We've got two, maybe three hours, and then the preacher is going to be here with those men from Wolf Hole," I said as I laid my head back on my saddle.

"What happened to Poke Joy? You kill him for that horse?"

"They killed him," I said; and I closed my eyes, noting the accusation which had been leveled against me. Well, it wasn't really an accusation; my partner was just funning me, but I still reminded myself the thought was there. I didn't want to talk about what had happened, and I think Ol' Slantface understood, because he didn't say any more. I wanted rest, even if it was only an hour.

As it turned out, I got two hours of rest, and then we broke up camp. The sun was on the eastern horizon, and there was still no sign of the scoundrels who had killed Poke Joy. We had our coffee, and I drank an extra cup for myself. Then we saddled up and crossed the river.

We were now in California, and it wasn't being called "The Golden State" just because we were carrying some of the ore either. James Marshall discovered gold during construction of Sutter's Mill nearly fifteen years earlier, and the California Gold Rush was on. There were other gold mines like Grass Valley, Placerville and Goldfield. All within one hundred miles of one another, and then there was Sutter's Mill at Coloma on the South Fork of the American River in Auburn Canyon, between Auburn and Placerville, the one that started it all. All those gold mines had me fantasizing as to whether it wouldn't be easier to let the preacher have the gold shipment and go dig our own. Then I remembered how we were constrained by time, and knew it would never work. Every minute it took from here on to get our gold shipment back to New

Orleans increased the chance the southern states would lose the war.

We left the river and headed into the Chocolate Mountains, only we didn't get far. Somehow those varmints had ridden around us and were waiting up in the hills. Their first barrage of gunfire lifted Private Loren from his saddle and grazed a few of our horses. Out in the wide open left us with no cover, so we tucked tail and headed back the way we came just as fast as our horses would carry us. Twenty minutes saw me hunkered down on the banks of the Colorado, waiting for the others to show up.

They filed in one or two at a time, leading the mules. Ol' Slantface was the first to make the river. He slid down the embankment, grabbed his rifle and came up beside me.

"I's hate losing a good man," he said as he looked over the ridge.

"I never figured they'd get here this quick," I offered up my excuse.

"They must have been right behind you de whole time."

I couldn't see any way such a thing was possible, but they were here, in fact they were ahead of us. What they had done just wasn't possible to my way of thinking, and I said as much. "They would have needed to wake up before I left their camp to get that far ahead of us," I managed.

"Then maybe dey ain't de same party. Maybe dey is still coming along behind us. Lord-have-mercy, I sure hope you is wrong, Dillon."

Getting up, Ol' Slantface walked to where the men were gathering at the river and started a conversation. When all was said and done, he posted four men on the other side of the river to watch our backs. The rest of us watched the California side. What I couldn't figure out was how I could be tricked so easily. Maybe at thirteen I wasn't as grown up as I figured. It hit me then, my birthday had come and gone while chasing the preacher half way around the globe. I was thirteen! With Poke Joy and Private Loren gone, we were short two men. Now there were only seven of us. I was counting myself lucky the number wasn't six. Who were the men who had ambushed us? It couldn't be the preacher; he hadn't enough time to get this far. He would be here soon, but he simply couldn't have gotten ahead of us. No rhyme or reason offered me an explanation which made any kind of sense. The party up ahead had to be another bunch.

"Well, it's possible," Ol' Slantface observed. "Gold is a mighty tempting thing right now. Even I would think of taking de stuff if'n it weren't so important for the war effort and the southern cause. If'n we don't git dis money back into de right hands in New Orleans, de war may be lost. May be lost already, long as dis trip is taking us, but we got's ta try."

"What are the right hands?" I asked solemnly.

"Judge Judge Pierre Rost. He owns de Destrehan Plantation on de river road. Dat family has handled all de major transactions fo' de south since before the United States became de United States."

"Wow," I exclaimed. "That must be an important family."

"Your name would have ta be George Washington ta be any more important in the doings of government."

"I'm wondering what we do now," I said, changing the subject.

"We wait'll de stars come out. Keep our eyes peeled, and we try ta sneak out of here in de dark."

"Yes, sir, that sounds like what we need to do," I admitted.

We waited then, and I got more sleep. We all did. They either had to come and get us, or we were going to sneak away from the river in the middle of the night. I slept the rest of the morning and awoke at the behest of Sergeant Ward. He told me everything I needed to watch for, and said to wake them if I saw anything. I wanted to, but I wasn't blessed with being able to spot anything at all. I didn't have to wake Ol' Slantface; a few hours later he got up on his own and took over. He told me to get more rest, but there was no real sleep in it.

I lay there with my hat over my face and wrestled with my future. What was it exactly that I was doing? I was setting myself up for failure ultimately—or was I? Learning how to track and kill a man was no life, not one that I could see, but I was not privy to what the future held in our great country, a country torn in two by war. I was not aware that the preacher was not the only man who might need killing. Had I thought about things, I would have reasoned the matter out right then, but a thirteen-year-old just doesn't have enough experience to do such a thing. I didn't have any idea, for instance, that after the war outlaws would run rampant on both sides.

There was no use I could see for what I was now learning, unless I someday became a hunted man. A man who knew his way around the west could lose any number of folks, if he knew the ins and outs of tracking. He could lead them astray, set traps for them in any number of ways; and right now it was up to us to do that very thing if we were going to make it home alive.

Those men up ahead had set a trap for us, and we'd ridden right in. Well, I could tell you a thing or two about my partner, Ol' Slantface. He was a man who could lay his own traps. In fact, as I lay there with my hat shading my face, I was certain that was exactly what he was thinking on. He was wondering just how he could draw in all of the men who were out there and beat them at their own game.

After waiting out the entire day, we saddled up and headed downstream toward the Mexican border. We traveled both sides of the river for a while, and then the fellows on the east bank crossed over to meet us. From there we rode south of the Chocolate Mountains, but stayed on the water; knowing animals would be coming to drink, Indians maybe and those men. When they would come was the question. Animals wouldn't come near the river until we had passed them by; however, men could lie in wait. For this reason we rode with caution and scouted every possible site.

When we found the right ambush site on a cliff overlooking the Colorado, Ol' Slantface positioned the men for the set-up. "From now on, we do de ambushing," he said; and we settled in.

We hadn't gone five miles downriver. The light of the moon was good and we could see for miles. What we couldn't figure was why neither assignment on either side of the river had seen anything. What were the men who ambushed us doing? What was the preacher doing? Were they working together?

We didn't have to wonder for long. In the distance we saw them coming. There were only seven of us now, and two of us were no more than boys. We counted twenty-one men and the preacher coming right along, slow and easy, pretty as you please. I thought to myself, I'll never see home again. Seven or eight or even ten of them, I figured we had a chance, but twenty-one men who wouldn't stop until they had the gold in their hands! That was too many. Right then I wished Captain Endicott was there to even things up with his men, but I knew they weren't coming, not any time soon. If they came at all, it would be to find our bodies so they would know what happened to the gold. That was my thinking until I learned how well those Confederate soldier boys could actually shoot, given the proper equipment.

Those men came on, and we were under orders to pick out a target and shoot only when Ol' Slantface shot and not before—his shot would be our signal. So I waited with Ol' Slantface positioned right below me on the cliff's edge. He leaned into his target and slowly squeezed his trigger. When he did, I sighted down my barrel and squeezed off a round, not hitting a thing. I had dusted a couple of those fellows a mite, but as for hitting one of them, my shot was a dead miss.

Suddenly there was nothing at all to shoot at. Three bodies lay on the riverbank, and the rest had taken cover. Eighteen—we had eighteen men and the preacher to worry about now. I began this count in my head not knowing if I should live or die. A boy can hope though and right then I began to hope the men I traveled with were able to withstand such a lopsided challenge.

They knew we were here; there was no ignoring such a fact. We had a good position on them, and as long as we had the light of the moon, we had them pinned down below. Come daylight, things would be worse for them. The firing had died down almost immediately; we had been ordered to save our ammo for a sure-fire shot. There was no sure-fire shot in the dark of night, but we had gotten three of them to get the ball rolling.

I watched intently as the shadows moved down below. They moved around under what little cover they had, mostly the scrub bushes lining the bank of the river. Everyone seemed to be on the west bank because the east bank was a cliff. Our location was a cliff also, but our cliff rose for three hundred feet into the night air, and the trail we had taken was one which could not be ascended from below, not as long as our guns covered the trail.

I saw someone move toward the river as if to fill his canteen, and four rifles barked simultaneously to bring him up short. The figure fell headlong into the water and floated away. Seventeen, there were now seventeen men left. I knew I wouldn't be any good with a rifle unless I had daylight, so I hadn't tried, but those soldier boys were primed and ready. All these weeks of chasing around the country after a thief, and now the thief had returned with an army of his own. My soldiers were men clean through. They had lost Private Loren and Poke Joy, and they didn't intend to lose another to the likes of the preacher. I couldn't blame them for their way of thinking. Private Loren had been a good soldier and Poke Joy had been nothing more than a child.

"Dillon, get some rest," I heard Ol' Slantface whisper back to my position, so I shucked my rifle and closed my eyes.

The night had been quiet, and at sunup I awoke to see Ol' Slantface taking aim on another man. Slowly he took up the slack on his trigger, and the rifle barked its command. Another man dropped into view and rolled down the riverbank to the edge of the water. Sixteen, we had their number whittled down to sixteen. We had them fairly pinned down, and there wasn't a thing they could do about it. They had no way out that I could see.

I was three hundred feet up in the rocks, and I wasn't sure I could hit anything shooting at a downward angle anyway, so I didn't waste my bullets. Now was not the time for experimenting. Thirty minutes later, one of the soldiers below me dropped another man, and their number became fifteen. Suddenly I began to have a ray of hope. They had gotten one of us in the beginning, but since then we had racked up six of their number. At that pace we could win, we had a chance!

Just then, I heard a boot grate on a rock up above me, and I spun just in time to cause the bullet meant for the back of my head to spit dirt in my face. I scratched and tore at my eyes, knowing I was likely dead, because I was certain the man up above me was the preacher I so wanted to kill.

With that realization, I palmed my father's six-gun and began firing through veiled eye-sight at the shadow up above. I heard a few grunts and then the body flew over me. The man thudded hard on the cliff behind me then sailed three hundred feet down, splashing into the river. I still couldn't see what had happened, but before I heard the splash, I heard his rifle tumble into the pit where I lay coming to rest beside me. When I finally got my eyes clear and was able to see again, I looked at the rifle. A spent shell was jammed in the ejection chamber. It wouldn't function again until the chamber was cleared. The preacher's repeating rifle had jammed and saved my life.

"You aw'right, Dillon?" Ol' Slantface wanted to know.

"Yes, sir," I said, my eyes in tears.

"You got Culpepper, boy, you sure as dickens got him. No man could live through a fall like dat, and ya put two, maybe three bullets into him."

"How did he get behind me?" I demanded.

"He must'uh floated downriver past us, den come in from behind. Deys no udder way," Slantface offered. "Stay right where you is, son. Just watch our backs, dere may be more. Keep your head down like before an' stay where you is. You'll do more good watching our backs," he said.

"Yes, sir," I replied, still stunned by my luck.

As I reloaded Pa's gun the thought suddenly occurred to me that Jeremiah Culpepper had gotten what he deserved. When he shot me, I had landed in the river, but I had jumped that way on purpose. His fall of three hundred feet or more was fitting. I had avenged my father's death and the death of my friend Poke Joy.

Another thought crossed my mind, something my mother used to always say before she died. "I believe in sunshine, I believe in rain, and I believe the Lord is my shepherd even if I am lost." Now, what triggered that memory for me was anybody's guess, but I hadn't thought much about my mother lately, and suddenly I felt ashamed.

Just then a rifle barked nearby, and another man was down. Thirteen, we had whittled them down to thirteen, and our position couldn't get any better. We waited for what seemed hours then, and finally we saw the white flag of surrender. Someone had tied a white cloth onto the end of a gun barrel and was waving it back and forth.

"Hello up there, we want a truce," the man was saying.

"Dillon, you watch our backs real good right now, dis may be a trick."

"Yes, sir," I said, and I turned to focus on the hill that lay behind us.

"What you want?" my partner yelled.

"We want you to let us go. There's no need for any more bloodshed. The preacher is dead. You done killed half the town."

"You can gather up de dead and ride out, but you go east, far as you can see," Slantface advised.

"That suits us fine. I want to get back to my business at Wolf Hole anyway before the rest of us get killed," the man said.

They gathered up then, and the chore took them all of two hours. They crossed the river upstream a ways and we could see them riding east. They were a sorry lot as they rode out with their heads hung low and bodies draped over saddles, but we had bested them and I had learned a little that day.

We had won. Now all we had to do was get back to San Diego Harbor. That was easier said than done. I wasn't sure we were clear of any Indian trouble yet, and carrying gold like we were, there was no guarantee we were clear of white men either. Then there was the ship ride. It was a long way back to New Orleans.

We waited right where we were until morning. In the early morning sun, we could see where the other men had camped, and they were now headed east, following the Castle Dome Plain toward Castle Dome Peak. Now, all we had to worry about was Indians and getting home. We saddled up and I stepped into the stirrup. I had me a souvenir, the preacher's jammed rifle, a .44 caliber Henry.

I kept his rifle all these years, and I want you to know there never was a more accurate weapon found, not in my sphere or in my possession. Why it jammed on him that day I will never know, but never in all my born days have I gotten that Henry to jam while using it.

Downriver the following morning, not far from the town of Yuma a body lay sprawled on the west bank, a man with three bullets in his chest, but still breathing. He was in unquestionably bad shape, not only filed with lead, but a broken leg and several broken ribs to boot. Two bullets were still lodged in his chest. His clothes were torn to doll rags, and he was missing one boot. He looked to be dead but for the fact his chest still rose and fell. A young woman from the village of Yuma came down to dip for water and found him. She found him, but if he lived or died would be up to his personal constitution; she could only do so much.

A doctor was sent for and the bullets were removed, but there was nothing more anyone could do. The doctor had been a veterinarian. There was no one else. The man was still unconscious, but he never quit breathing on his own. He didn't eat, nor did he drink. All the woman could do was squeeze water from a washcloth into his open mouth so he didn't dry out too much. No one knew who the man was; only that he had been shot and left for dead, yet somehow he had floated downriver to the village.

Chapter 16

A week-long ride saw us back to San Diego, where we found Captain Endicott and his men waiting. We boarded a ship called the *Proclamation* and sailed out of the harbor in late August. The weather around San Diego wasn't something I minded at all, considering we were now in the middle of summer. For that matter, the desert east of San Diego hadn't been bad either, not until you got high up into the mountains; only then had it been rather chilly.

We rode the ship quietly, keeping guard on our gold, cleaning our weapons, week in and week out. You have no idea what salt water will do to a weapon, or how fast one will rust one until you leave it unattended aboard a ship for any length of time. I found if, after cleaning mine real well, I smeared grease up and down the barrel, the salt air couldn't get to the metal, and when I discovered my little trick, the rest of the men followed suit. This made me feel good, but we used up a whole barrel of grease keeping our weapons from rusting up. When we made landfall in New Orleans nine weeks later, our weapons were still in good shape.

As we sailed into New Orleans, the weather was fixing to blow. I had heard the term "hurricane," but I had never experienced one, though I was about to. We had expected a blockade in the gulf port, but the Yankee Fleet must have pulled out in order to get their vessels to safety. We had a dickens of a time just getting our stock off board the *Proclamation* in such turbulent weather.

New Orleans was like St. Louis from what I had seen; boats in the harbor everywhere you looked, yet many of them were deep water sailing vessels. There were steamboats, ships, flat boats, little boats and big ones. However, with the bad weather blowing in, most of them had departed for open sea or upriver to get away from what Ol' Slantface said was the storm surge. "Dem boats what don't seek cover are liable ta end up as tree houses," my friend opined. Such a declaration sent shivers down my spine. Just what was a hurricane anyway?

Usually there were many more colored folks hanging around on the docks for loading and unloading in New Orleans, but this labor was meant for the express purpose of moving cargo aboard a ship, or off-loading it. They didn't do anything else. Some fellows would play a harmonica as the men worked. Others would call a cadence and sing. Their labor was all timed to music. As we took our beasts off the boat, I noticed that even the laborers had disappeared. I had witnessed their like in St. Louis, and I had seen them when we boarded in the harbor at the beginning of our journey, but they were nowhere to be seen on this day.

We finally got unloaded with our horses, mules and gear. Ol' Slantface asked directions of a local man to the Destrehan Plantation. We mounted up with our Confederate Army escort and headed up river to the home of the Judge. He was our contact man, and he would take the gold off our hands. We laughed and joked as we rode, but we were getting wet too. A fine spray was coming down as we plodded toward our destination. I say coming down, it was coming more sideways than straight down. Later, this light mist would turn to a torrential downpour, flooding everything for miles around.

The colorful breath of flowers; all had bloomed and now had left the garden. Wind-driven rain removed the last petals of summer, while honeysuckle on the vine floated on the stormy tempest, which at times, parted the curtains of the Destrehan Plantation on River Road as wind gusts pushed through the open sash windows. Louise Destrehan Rost sat by her window clutching her heaving breast, trying to restrain her broken heart, fearful the organ would tear from her chest at any moment. The year was now 1863, and yellow fever had stricken much of the south in the years since 1853. Death had paid a visit to the Destrehan Plantation. Her two children were gone! Both son and daughter, so full of life only a few months earlier were now in their final resting place.

She had worried about Emile, her oldest, for he was fighting for the south and she had been almost certain she would receive notice that he had been killed in a battle somewhere far off, but death had struck right here at home instead.

What God-awful reason was there for children dying before their parents, before their fragile lives had even begun? How the death of a child could take such a beautiful place as the Destrehan Plantation and turn its beauty into the very halls of Hell! Son and daughter ripped from her bosom in what was supposed to be the pinnacle of her life, the part where her children's dreams would come true, where a mother's happiness was measured by their happiness, where children multiplied into grandchildren down the long years.

Now, with all she believed about God being kind and gentle, forgiving and just, He had imposed upon her a life worse than death. A sentence she could not comprehend. She struggled just to breathe of late.

Louise Destrehan Rost understood God knew every hair upon your head, God knew your needs before you did, God knew the very hour you were to depart this world. What possible justification could He have in taking her two precious children, innocent darlings who had done nothing wrong? She had done nothing wrong; she was a good Christian, untainted by sinful habitude which seemed so common in humans. Louise Destrehan Rost had lived as only a faithful servant could. If as she believed, all life was preordained and your time of death known only to God Himself, God was going to have to answer to her when the time came for her to meet Him, because in her mind, God had in essence betrayed her.

Lydia had been the most beautiful of young ladies, with a golden fleece of hair, a never-ending smile and an unmatched zeal for life. She understood her place in the world as no other young lady of her time possibly could. Lydia, in all of her seventeen years, had never been discourteous; never embarrassed her family or herself, and she had developed an etiquette which surpassed even that of her mother. She would have made a grand first lady.

Her older brother, Henri, had been a robust young man; a spitting image of his father, and the most respected young gentleman in Southern Louisiana. He was already engaged at the time of his passing; to Molly O'Hara, who had died only three days behind the love of her life. At six foot three, he had commanded respect and carried himself as a gentleman. Always courteous and always thinking of others, he had begun his own law practice. Now too, he was gone.

There could be no justifiable reason for this visit from the Angel of Death. Hence, Louise Destrehan Rost teetered precariously upon the cliff of insanity. Her entire reason for existence had been torn from her motherly grasp and her family decimated. Death had snuck in the back door of their great home on the river road, a home which now stood in all its majesty awaiting orders from the life-giving beauty which surrounded the grand structure.

Louise noted in her thoughts; nature does give orders, every day man has to contend with God's nature, man's movements and responses are in direct relation to what he encounters in nature. She noted her findings on a separate sheet of paper and put it in a drawer to dry.

Mattie had lost her children too, but so had many folks. Mattie, who was a pillar of strength, still waited on Louise and gave her comfort. The servant of the house was anything but a servant, in her own mind. Mattie was family, although she was of another color and race. Whenever anyone needed an answer or advice, they came to Mattie; even more so now that Louise was suffering so. If she didn't already possess the answer, she would see either the judge or Lady Rost and return with the requested information.

A hurricane was blowing in from the gulf and the weather was getting rough, the final swansong for any honeysuckle still left upon the vine. There was nothing to do but wait the storm out. Judge Rost had traveled to Baton Rouge to visit with his friend Zachary Taylor because the gold shipment needed for buying war supplies had never materialized. The War Between the States was raging and the Federals had now taken Vicksburg.

The door pushed open and Mattie stepped into the room with a tray, upon it a glass of milk. She recognized immediately that her lady was in distress so she comforted her in the only way she knew how. "De Law'd, He knows what for He takin' dem young'ns. Now you quit'cha cryin' and drink yo milk."

"Mattie, I can't. I can hardly breathe," Louise complained.

"Ma'am, you bes' do as I say's or I got's ta tell de Judge when he git home!"

"Oh Mattie, help me, Mattie. I'm afraid I hate God. I can no longer worship a God who is so cruel."

"Mercy, mercy, don' go an' say such a thing. Why He's li'ble ta strike you dead where you sit, and I can't be bur'in you for such nonsense. Now drink what milk I brung ya."

Lifting the glass slowly to her lips, Louise took a few swallows of the fresh milk and acknowledged its wholesomeness, for the cool refreshment was indeed good.

"Mattie, how can I go on? I have lost my only reason for living. What am I to do?"

"My, my, listen t'ya now. I done los' mine too, but'cha cain't quit on de Judge. Why, he done had his heart broke too. He cain't show it none 'cause he got so many folks dependin' on him for everthang; why, he got no time ta grieve, just like I got no time ta grieve. What's done is done, and we ain't going t' bring nobody back. If'n we could, why it'd be done already, wouldn't it."

"You've put your finger on it, Mattie."

"I got my finger on nothin."

"I mean you are right. The judge is too busy to let the devil get the better of him. All I do is sit around this old house and fret about what I've lost, and look at me. I'm a nervous wreck! You don't have time to worry like me, and look at you; why, you are as strong as ever. I've got to get busy. All I'm doing is cooking in my own pot of self-pity stew, and if I'm not careful, I'll become a part of that debris of humanity which is worth absolutely nothing."

"Now ya's talkin' sense, my lady. Jes what ya goin' to be busy 'bout?"

"I don't yet know, but it will come to me."

Tipping up her glass, Louise finished her milk and placed the glass upon the silver tray. Then she turned back toward the window and looked out upon the graying grounds of her beloved plantation.

"Mattie, have Jude cut fresh flowers from the garden and bring them inside before the storm gets any worse. I think I should like to smell their aroma one last time before this storm wipes them out."

"Yes'm," Mattie said, as she removed the tray from the table and started for the doorway. The Destrehan slave known as Mattie was indeed a strong-spirited woman in her late thirties, a woman of dark skin who carried herself as if she were royalty. In Mattie's mind, she was no less than royalty, for no one else could match her position on the plantation. She listened to the judge rant about the day's activities and to Mrs. Rost as she managed the household from day to day, and Mattie, nine times out of ten, issued the orders for the family. She knew with every fiber of her being that no one could replace her and do as fine a job. Mattie was swelling with pride, for no other slave she knew had attained her stature in any family. Her equal was nowhere to be had. Not in Louisiana or anywhere else in the South; except for that cook President Lincoln had in the White House, no one was thought of as her equal.

Later that evening while everyone was asleep, when all of the lamps in the big house had been turned out, a lone candle glowed. Louise Destrehan Rost glided quietly toward her desk and eased herself into her writing chair, placing her candle down lightly on the upper left-hand side of the leather writing surface, where the light would have the most benefit. Opening the upper right-hand drawer, she slid out some stationery and began to write poetry. She held the paper still with her left hand and took up her pen with the right, long slender fingers which the Mayor of New Orleans had once described as "the most beautiful hands he'd ever had the opportunity to kiss." Her hand was deceptively young, for it had never known the pleasures or the rigors of hard work.

If you looked at the figure sitting across the room from the big open windows of her upper bedroom you would behold a very young and rare beauty. She rubbed her eyes for a moment with her always-present kerchief, eyes that were swollen from weeping which carried heavy rings of exhaustion beneath them. Folding her handkerchief in her left hand beneath her long, slender ring-covered fingers, she soaked the pen in her inkwell and began to write.

I watch the tree limbs break and fall.
I hear the floor creaking in the hall.
Trees drop their leaves all through the fall.
Fate reigns supreme within us all.

Toward death my body hastens,
The evidence of my birth,
Yet must I yield up my soul?
Then of what value is it?

I am taught of God,
And taught of Satan,
Even at a casual glance,
Both obviously want what is mine.

To my knowledge I have not seen,
Nor have I heard from my soul.
I am told the day long I have one,
Yet, where pray tell is it?

Deny yourself, abstain from sin,
Refrain, do without, forbear and sacrifice
In hope that God will find favor,
Yet Judgment Cometh!

Presently, she laid down her pen and stared at what she had just written. The words jumped at her from the page, as if with a life of their own, yet they were all wrong. Such a morbid poem. Tearing the poem to shreds, she picked up her pen and started over.

Not long ago,
A baby in your nest,
So sweet innocent a beau,
Now life had torn this child from her.

Another one came,
A balance of the best,
So sweet innocent a girl,
Life, so cruel had torn another from her.

There could be no loss so great,
As to rend her heart to pieces,
The loss of both her children,
Yet through a miracle she still breathed.

What life is this?
To rip one's heart to shreds,
Then paste it back together,
And fill it full of dreads.

Another day beckons,
But there, light sheds no joy,
Another breath now taken,
Her girl and little boy.

Satan calls his roll,
Yet somehow two are missing,
The girl and little boy,
Are now with Jesus whispering.

Awkwardly mother reaches,
For a doll which once was played,

And Jumping Jacks for the boy,
Her sentence in Hell shan't be stayed.

Pray tell,
Someone needs her,
But who in God's name?
A boy or little girl,
Father in Heaven, Hollowed be thy name.

Louise Destrehan Rost trembled, as she placed the paper upside down on her desk for no one to witness. She placed her pen back in the inkwell and shuddered, her realization of what God had done for her moved her so. God had allowed her children to be taken so that she might be a stronger person. He had ordained it, yet she teetered so dangerously close to the edge.

Clutching at the vast barrenness which now overflowed from her heart, she made her way over to her bed and buried her face in the soft tear stained satin pillows. The satin sheet now wrinkled and disturbed, she writhed in agony upon her bed for several minutes, praising God and cursing the Devil! It was their doing, their war against one another which was responsible for this. It had always been so and always would remain, but God had not done this, Satan had. God would never do such a thing.

Louise quivered as she lay atop her bed allowing the waves of spiritual relief to overtake her physically. She could have no more children, but God would provide children for her. "Forgive me Lord, for being short sighted," she prayed. How she did not know, yet by the time she fell asleep she understood what God had in store for the Destrehan Plantation. The evidence was all around her, yet she had ignored it just as everyone else had.

The ride to the plantation took us about two hours, in which we got completely drenched. I had seen storms in Missouri, but they were nothing like this. This far south, Spanish moss grew everywhere, resting upon every tree limb. A few clumps of the stuff blew loose from its mooring overhead and landed on me, or I never would have asked what the substance was. On this day it was a special nuisance. I learned about palmetto bushes and palm trees while thinking, but for all the rain, New Orleans would be a nice place to live.

When we arrived at the Destrehan Plantation I learned what a mansion was. We walked our horses cautiously up the long drive, which was lined with two-hundred-year-old "live oaks." The trees sheltered us a good deal from the rain. I learned they stayed green year round. Whoever heard of an oak tree which stayed green year round? Apparently they did, because we were deep into the fall, and they were still green from what I could see.

The lady of the house, Louise Destrehan Rost, sent a slave named Shemp out to us to show us where to shelter our horses. Then he led us all into the house from the back. We brought the gold in with us, and Shemp departed. The servant of the house, who was named Mattie, mustered a good deal of help on the back porch which used brick flooring from one end to the other then ushered us into a sitting room, where we could all dry off by the fireplace. She had the slaves bring us blankets to help us get warm and dry. She had other servants stoke the fire in the parlor until it was good and hot.

This went on for near two hours before the lady of the house sent for Captain Endicott and Lieutenant Trumann. She ignored Ol' Slantface, who everyone assumed was our leader, and asked for the two officers only. This didn't bother my friend, as he was used to southern ways and said he would not disgrace such an esteemed southern lady of position. Well, I didn't know what esteemed meant, but I was happy Ol' Slantface didn't mind. In fact, it seemed to me he was relieved by the course of matters and didn't worry none about situations he couldn't control.

When the men returned about thirty minutes later, they were not happy. "The judge has gone to Baton Rouge, to the home of Zachary Taylor. He's not expected back until next week. With this storm brewing, it may be longer. The swamps between here and there will be impassible while the storm blows."

"What are we de do?" Ol' Slantface asked.

"We are guests of the house until Judge Rost returns. Until then we can do nothing.

"If'n we don't git dis gold into his hands soon, de war will be lost."

"It may already be lost," Captain Endicott retorted.

"What do you mean?"

"Grant has the Confederate forces effectively divided, and the east-west supply line for the Confederate Army has been shut off. I fear it's only a matter of time. We were lucky to debark in New Orleans. If not for the storm, the Yankees would have rounded us up. They have the town quartered. They have Baton Rouge and they have captured Vicksburg."

"Dat's not good news, Caps."

"No, it isn't."

"We have to do something; we can't just sit here," Lieutenant Trumann interrupted.

"What do you propose we do, Lieutenant?" the Captain wanted to know.

"I have no idea," Trumann said.

"We've nothing but time on our hands until this storm blows over, which means we have time to come up with some ideas," Captain Endicott suggested.

Just then Mattie came into the room and said, "The lady of the house would like to see the little boy."

"Just de boy?" Slantface questioned.

"Yes, sir."

"Dillon, go wid her and be on your best manners," my friend advised.

I followed her through the house to a large sitting room at the far end, where the shutters were closed against the storm. The wind came howling from all directions. The room was wallpapered with sailing ships and men of the sea, while curtains hung all the way down to the cypress plank floor from every window. They shaded the room with the color of dusk. Mrs. Rost was sitting at a writing desk and turned to look at me when I came in.

"Thank you, Mattie, you may go now."

The maidservant turned and left the room, and Mrs. Rost addressed me. "You may have a seat, young man. What's your name?"

"My name is Dillon Childs, Ma'am."

"What on earth are you doing with such a party of soldiers and reprobates?"

"I'm not sure what reprobate means, Ma'am."

"Lucifer Deal, that is what I mean; why, the man deals in human flesh, and he doesn't care how he gets his slaves! He has forever been known in these parts as the devil himself, he deals in the black market," she iterated.

"Yes, Ma'am, I'm aware of my partner's past, but I think he might be changing for the better. I call him Slantface."

"Slantface. His name is Lucifer Deal."

"He likes Ol' Slantface, ma'am."

The lady paused for a moment and a smile came to her lips, lips which hadn't smiled in a long, long time, if my guess was correct. "So, you have tamed the Ol' sidewinder."

"Yes, Ma'am, he prefers Slantface to Lucifer," I said, having forgotten his real name until she reminded me.

I was sitting in a small chair beside her desk. "How did you come to travel with the likes of Ol' Slantface?" she took on naturally.

"You want the entire story?"

"Yes Dillon, I want the entire story."

I told her then from the beginning; the night I overheard Slantface and his men talking about kidnapping children off the streets of St. Louis, to their holding them in the cabin, and my sister. I told her about being shot by the preacher and his men; how we both recovered in Tennessee and set out together. I told her how I had taken revenge and how we had gotten the gold back. I left nothing out. Her face registered horror several times, but she was a lady, and she recovered quickly.

"So your father is gone and his death has been avenged?"

"Yes, Ma'am," I said.

"How old are you, Dillon?"

"I'm thirteen," I replied.

"You've gone as far as you are going with those men. You have a home here for as long as you want one, and I'm going to send for your sister. If she can't come here, we'll go get her."

"Ma'am, I appreciate your thoughtfulness, but..."

"There are no buts, young Dillon. You will make the Destrehan Plantation your home. You're going to need your education, which has been sorely lacking these last months. Here, you shall receive the finest education money can buy. You will be properly educated and taught how to be a gentleman; I won't have it any other way."

Well, I just stared at her. I was willing to live here, but so many things were left unanswered. I needed to know more, but the lady of the house was suddenly as silent as me. She picked up a bell and rang it. Shortly Mattie showed up, and Mrs. Rost gave her new instructions.

"Mattie, young Dillon is going to be a ward here for some time to come. I want you to escort him to Henri's old bedroom and make him comfortable. He will be dining with us from now on."

"Yes, Ma'am. Come with me," Mattie said, and we were away. I followed Mattie to the far end of the house upstairs, and she opened the door to a room. There, she opened the curtains and peeled back the blankets. "Woul' you like dem clothes wash and clean, Masta Dillon?"

"I don't know, I..."

"You git dem dirty clothes off d'is minute; I'll send for a bath and you'll get cleaned too," she instructed. It was then I saw the bathtub in the corner and realized she intended to scrub months of trail dirt off of me. I have to admit I was slow to move for several reasons, not the least of which was, I had never been scrubbed by anyone since I was a baby.

"You go behind de curtain and git dem clothes off."

I did as I was told, and then she said, "Don't you dare lay on that bed afore we gits you clean either."

I stood behind that curtain, naked as a jaybird, until she came back in the room with some helpers who were carrying buckets of fresh clean water. Young girls they were, and I was never so embarrassed in my life. They made three trips up and down the stairs, delivering the water to the tub. Mattie told me to get in, so I didn't argue. It was cold at first, but it felt good to get the dirt scrubbed off. While she scrubbed me and washed my hair, she laid down the rules of the house, and suddenly I had the feeling that everything she was doing was routine. She was explaining everything in detail, what the household was used to. This bath was an improvement over my last one, as it had been a swim in the ocean.

I was to get a bath every morning before breakfast, which was served at five-thirty sharp. I was to wear a clean suit of clothes every day, and if I somehow got my clothes dirty, I was to change and start over. Lunch would be served at noon and supper at six. I was to study with the lady of the house until she was certain I was ready for school. Suddenly I had a life of luxury I had never known, and not a clue as to why.

At first I had feelings of being kidnapped again, but as I got cleaned up, I began to look around the bedroom, which was to be mine. A feeling of comfort came over me and I knew I was going to stay, for a while anyway. Jenny should be with me, but how to retrieve her seemed a daunting task now that the Federals owned the Mississippi from stem to stern.

As Mattie bathed me proper, the storm really began to rage. The wind kicked up several notches, and then there was lightning and thunder. The storm was made to order for anyone not wanting to venture outside after dark. There would be no argument from me; I was shaking in my own skin half the time, not from cold water, but from all of the close lightning strikes.

I looked my room over some more while Mattie scrubbed me clean, and I liked what I saw. I had my own desk, I had a big four poster bed, and the room was bigger than our whole cabin back in Missouri, if you took the porch off it. The bed was covered in a fine dark blue blanket with gold trim, which I later learned was a comforter with matching curtains. The comforter was not the comfort it should have been, because I was not allowed to lay upon it.

The shutters on my windows remained closed because of the storm, but I imagined how wonderful the view would be once they were opened. I had an armoire for hanging clothes and another rather large dresser and mirror. The floor was a medium stained finish, covered with a large rug and several smaller ones. The walls were hung with paintings of ships, along with one of the Destrehan Plantation itself. I studied this one and marveled at the detail. The Destrehan's were really rich.

When Mattie finished, she made me stand up so she could towel me dry. I was embarrassed at the prospect, but I got through it all right. She told me what for when I showed any sign or lack of understanding. She ran the Destrehan household with an iron fist. I was not going to be able to rule her. For that matter, I was not going to be able to rule my own destiny, either. Seemed to me everyone else was busy doing that for me.

Mattie had another servant bring in a fresh change of clothes for me, and she informed me that they had belonged to Mrs. Rost's son who had died of yellow fever. Her daughter had also died, and suddenly I understood why she was adopting me. She missed her children. Well, I missed my mother and father as much as she missed them, so maybe we could help each other. I was missing Jenny too!

When I went downstairs for dinner, the men who were still guests in the house didn't even recognize me, I had cleaned up swell. They had never seen me in such a condition.

"Lord have mercy, is that you, Dillon?" Captain Endicott asked as I sat down to the table.

"Yes, Sir," I responded.

"I would have never recognized you. You look fine," he said. Then Mrs. Rost came into the dining room and took her seat at the head of the long table. Everybody got up, so I did too, although I didn't know what for. Once she sat back down, we all sat back down.

The food was brought in then, and everyone was served. "Captain Endicott, will you please say grace?"

"Yes, Ma'am," he replied.

We all bowed our heads then as the Captain said grace for everyone in the room. It was a fine meal, and no one spoke a word until the lady of the house asked a question.

"Slantface, is it?" She said braving a smile at the former slave trader.

"It is," the old fellow responded.

"I must say you surprised me. Dillon here tells me you purchased young O'Queda from servitude aboard a ship you were traveling on."

"I did."

"How much did you pay?"

"Three hundred dollars," Slantface offered.

"You've had quite an adventure, the lot of you. It may not be over." Pausing, she added, "I want to thank you," she cleared her throat here, "Slantface, for all you have done for young Dillon, but we can all agree he's better off living here, where he can be properly educated and prepared for the life he has ahead."

"Dat would be a fine undertaking, Ma'am," he said. He winked at me then with his one good eye, and I knew we would be parting ways. I was sad, knowing my friend and companion would soon be gone, but happy that he was fine with the arrangement.

"As for O'Queda," here she pointed to the young man who sat across from her. "I will give you back your three hundred dollars. Dillon is going to need a companion. I vow to you, he will not be a slave in my household; I am purchasing his freedom."

"Dat won't be necessary, Mrs. Rost. I's already purchased his freedom. Dey's no need ta do the deed twice," Ol' Slantface countered.

"Dillon is correct; you are a changed man. Whatever possessed you to try to kidnap orphans off the streets of St. Louis, might I ask?"

"Greed, nothing but bloody, filthy greed. If'n you'll forgive an old dog, ma'am," he answered. "A way of life is coming ta an end. I's only trying to hang onto ta only life I knew. I knows better now."

"What will you do?" Louise Destrehan Rost was elegant and to the point.

"I's not sure, but I intend ta make sure de gold gets delivered where it's supposed ta go, den I will look around and see where de wind blows." My friend was using his best English here.

"You are welcome here any time, Mr. Deal. Dillon is fond of you, although I can't say exactly why. I know he has learned many things from you over the last few months, including some which he must no doubt unlearn." She stared long and hard at me as she said this. "I would take it kindly if you would stop in whenever you are in New Orleans, if for no other reason than to say hello to Dillon and O'Queda, or have a bite to eat."

"I would be honored, Ma'am."

"I will need a good ship's captain to take me upriver to retrieve Dillon's sister; do you know of one?"

"Capt'n Grimes would be de man you's looking for. He drops in at Belle Grove Plantation when he's dis far south. He may be dere now," Ol' Slantface advised.

"Captain Grimes, the Confederate mail runner for the south?"

"Yes, Ma'am, I's never met him, but de one and de same," my friend responded.

"I see; well, maybe he is the sort of man I will need; he certainly doesn't seem to have any problem getting past the Yankees. The newspapers say he has escaped from them several times already," Louise Rost observed out loud.

"He and dat fellow Mark Twain, they grew up together in Hannibal, Missouri. If anybody can pull off such a shenanigan, Cap'm Grimes can do it," he added.

We ate then, and no one said much else. I seemed to remember the name Captain Grimes from somewhere in my past, but I couldn't quite put a finger on it. When the meal was over, the men retired to the drawing room and O'Queda was escorted to his new quarters along with me. I could hear the scrubbing and the complaining going on in the next room, and I laughed. I knew what O'Queda was getting, and I also knew he didn't take a liking to it none. I slipped under the covers and suddenly I remembered who Captain Grimes was. He had rescued me from the swamp, he had saved my life! I never got a chance to meet him because he left before I woke up. I went to sleep that night with a real smile on my face for the first time in a long time.

Three days later, Ol' Slantface took off with the army and made a concerted effort to locate Judge Pierre Rost on his way back from Baton Rouge. I heard all about it when the judge arrived home a few days later.

Now and again, I run into Ol' Slantface down on the wharf. The war was lost and all the slaves were freed, but the real cruelty was, most of them didn't know how to survive without being told what to do and where to go. They had been given orders so long they didn't know how to think for themselves, their newfound freedom was a sentence of life-long poverty in most cases. Through no fault of the judge, the gold never was delivered to the right party to purchase weapons needed for the south, so that had plenty to do with the outcome of the war.

Ol' Slantface owns his own shipping company now. He became a sea-faring man when the war was over, and he rides the waves like the free spirit captain he is. Someday soon, when my studies are finished, I shall go with him on a trip, but that is another story.

About the Author

Other novels from John T. Wayne include:

CATFISH JOHN
THE TREASURE DEL DIABLO
BLOOD ONCE SPILLED

CPSIA information can be obtained
at www.ICGtesting.com
Printed in the USA
FSOW01n0310130317
31665FS